A Christmas Star

Judith Keim

BOOKS BY JUDITH KEIM

The Talking Tree (The Hartwell Women –1)
Sweet Talk (The Hartwell Women – 2)
Straight Talk (The Hartwell Women – 3)
Baby Talk (The Hartwell Women – 4)
The Hartwell Women Series – (Boxed Set)
Breakfast at The Beach House Hotel –1
Lunch at The Beach House Hotel – 2
Dinner at The Beach House Hotel – 3
Christmas at The Beach House Hotel – 4
Fat Fridays (Fat Fridays Group – 1)
Sassy Saturdays (Fat Fridays Group – 2)
Secret Sundays (Fat Fridays Group – 3)
Finding Me – A Salty Key Inn Book – 1
Finding My Way – A Salty Key Inn Book – 2
Finding Love – A Salty Key Inn Book – 3
Finding Family – A Salty Key Inn Book – 4
A Christmas Star – A Seashell Cottage Book – 1
Going Home – A Chandler Hill Book – 1 (Early 2019)
Coming Home – A Chandler Hill Book – (Late 2019)
Home at Last – A Chandler Hill Book – (Early 2020)
Winning BIG – a little love story for all ages
For more information: http://amzn.to/2jamIaF

CHILDREN'S BOOKS BY J. S. KEIM

The Hidden Moon (The Hidden Moon Series – 1)
Return to the Hidden Moon (The Hidden Moon Series – 2)
Trouble on the Hidden Moon (The Hidden Moon Series – 3)
Kermit Greene's World
For more information: http://amzn.to/2qlqKMI

PRAISE FOR JUDITH KEIM'S NOVELS

THE BEACH HOUSE HOTEL SERIES

"*Love the characters in this series. This series was my first introduction to Judith Keim. She is now one of my favorites. Looking forward to reading more of her books.*"

BREAKFAST AT THE BEACH HOUSE HOTEL *is an easy, delightful read that offers romance, family relationships, and strong women learning to be stronger. Real life situations filter through the pages. Enjoy!*"

LUNCH AT THE BEACH HOUSE HOTEL – "*This series is such a joy to read. You feel you are actually living with them. Can't wait to read the latest one.*"

DINNER AT THE BEACH HOUSE HOTEL – "*A Terrific Read! As usual, Judith Keim did it again. Enjoyed immensely. Continue writing such pleasantly reading books for all of us readers.*"

CHRISTMAS AT THE BEACH HOUSE HOTEL – "*Not Just Another Christmas Novel. This is book number four in the series and my introduction to Judith Keim's writing. I wasn't disappointed. The characters are dimensional and engaging. The plot is well crafted and advances at a pleasing pace. The Florida location is interesting and warming. It was a delight to read a romance novel with mature female protagonists. Ann and Rhoda have life experiences that enrich the story. It's a clever book about friends and extended family. Buy copies for your book group pals and enjoy this seasonal read.*"

THE HARTWELL WOMEN

"This was an EXCELLENT series. When I discovered Judith Keim, I read all of her books back to back. I thoroughly enjoyed the women Keim has written about. They are believable and you want to just jump into their lives and be their friends! I can't wait for any upcoming books!"

"I fell into Judith Keim's Hartwell Women series and have read & enjoyed all of her books in every series. Each centers around a strong & interesting woman character and their family interaction. Good reads that leave you wanting more."

THE FAT FRIDAYS GROUP

"Excellent story line for each character, and an insightful representation of situations which deal with some of the contemporary issues women are faced with today."

"I love this author's books. Her characters and their lives are realistic. The power of women's friendships is a common and beautiful theme that is threaded throughout this story."

THE SALTY KEY INN SERIES

FINDING ME – *"I thoroughly enjoyed the first book in this series and cannot wait for the others! The characters are endearing with the same struggles we all encounter. The setting makes me feel like I am a guest at The Salty Key Inn...relaxed, happy & light-hearted! The men are yummy and the women strong. You can't get better than that! Happy Reading!"*

FINDING MY WAY- *"Loved the family dynamics as well as uncertain emotions of dating and falling in love. Appreciated the morals and strength of parenting throughout. Just couldn't put this book down."*

FINDING LOVE – "*I waited for this book because the first two was such good reads. This one didn't disappoint.... Judith Keim always puts substance into her books. This book was no different, I learned about PTSD, accepting oneself, there is always going to be problems but stick it out and make it work. Just the way life is. In some ways a lot like my life. Judith is right, it needs another book and I will definitely be reading it. Hope you choose to read this series, you will get so much out of it.*"

OTHER COMMENTS

"*Always love books written by Judith Keim. From these strong women who go through lots of difficulties and adventure to the Florida beach hotel books. Every book is entertaining and fun to read with plenty of excitement and surprises.*
"*I was first introduced to Judith Keim's books with her Beach House series and since then look forward to each new book from this author. Her stories draw you in so you become invested in the lives of her characters and want to know what comes next.*"

A Christmas Star

A Seashell Cottage Book - 1

Judith Keim

Wild Quail Publishing

This is a work of fiction. Names, characters, places, public or private institutions, corporations, towns, and incidents are the product of the author's imagination or are used fictitiously. Any resemblance to actual events, locales, or persons, living or dead, is coincidental.

No part of this book may be reproduced or transmitted in any form or by any electronic or mechanical means, including information storage and retrieval systems, without permission in writing from the author, except by a reviewer who may quote brief passages in a review. This book may not be resold or uploaded for distribution to others.

Wild Quail Publishing
PO Box 171332
Boise, ID 83717-1332

ISBN# 978-0-9992448-4-5

Dedication

In loving memory of Marie Louise "Weezie" Williams, my great-aunt, who always believed the real spirit of Christmas was in people sharing and making the wishes of others come true.
I still believe it.

CHAPTER ONE

On the Gulf Coast of Florida, Noelle North walked along the white, sandy beach that lined the shore like the fur on her slippers back home. The sun's heat washed over her, hugging her with its warmth on this early December morning. She unzipped her light jacket and lifted her arms to the blue sky, welcoming the day with an embrace. She had a whole six weeks of freedom from work and her dismal life back home. It was worth every penny of her savings.

Her family had wanted her to stay in Boston with them for the holidays, but Noelle knew she couldn't endure another Christmas of everyone feeling sorry for her. Two years ago on Christmas Day, her ex-fiancé, Alexander Cabot, had left her waiting at the church on her wedding day, while he'd taken off with another woman, his best friend's wife. She'd wanted to die of embarrassment. Even now, thinking of that humiliation, a shudder shook her shoulders, and her stomach filled with acid.

The one thing that had helped her keep going throughout the healing process was the conviction she'd never fall for a rich guy again. Besides, at thirty-two and with her unfortunate track record with men, she was pretty sure she was destined to be single for the rest of her life. The thought didn't bother her as much as it used to. Why should it? She had the freedom to come and go as she pleased, nobody was around to tell her what she could or couldn't do, and evenings after a hard day of work at the New Life Assisted-Living Community were blissfully quiet.

Noelle stopped walking and gazed out over the water. Waves rolled toward her in a steady pattern, greeting the shore with a kiss and pulling away like a shy child. Above her, seagulls wheeled in circles, their cries shrill in the stillness of the early morning. She watched as a group of sandpipers darted toward the water's edge, dipped their beaks into the sand for whatever little morsel they could catch, and continued on their way, leaving tiny footprints behind.

A flash of black caught her attention. She turned to see a big dog galloping toward her, yellow tennis ball in his mouth. She braced herself to greet him and then chuckled as the dog circled and ran right by her toward a small figure farther down the beach.

She walked on, watching with interest as the dog ran into the water and came out again carrying the wet ball in his mouth. As she came closer, she saw that the person throwing the ball was a boy whom she guessed was seven or eight.

The boy smiled at her as she approached.

"Your dog is a very good catcher," Noelle said. "What's his name?"

"Duke," the boy said. The dog, hearing his name, came and sat by him.

"And what's your name?" Noelle asked, thinking the boy with dark red hair, bright green eyes, and freckles was one of the cutest kids she'd ever seen.

"Silas. Silas Bellingham." He studied her. "Who are you? And why aren't you working?"

She grinned. "I'm Noelle North, and I'm not working because I'm on vacation for the next month or so." She glanced around. "Are you here by the water on your own?"

"Naw. My great-grandmother's over there. See?" He pointed to a woman sitting in a wheelchair on the porch of a sizeable house overlooking the beach.

Noelle smiled and lifted a hand in greeting, but the woman didn't wave back.

"See you later," the boy said, and ran toward his great-grandmother.

Noelle watched him go, thinking of all her friends' children back home. Of the women who had stuck together through everything since college, she was the only one who was unmarried and without children. She'd always wanted a large family, but that didn't seem possible now. With no prospects of a husband in sight, she would be lucky to have even one baby.

Trying to fight off depression, Noelle resumed walking. It was bad enough to have been dumped at the altar on Christmas, but that day was also her birthday. With a name like Noelle, she'd always felt the holiday season was something extra special, almost magical, in her life. Until two years ago, that is. Now, Christmas trees, Christmas decorations, and especially Christmas music were nauseating to her. She walked on wishing her grandmother were alive. From an early age, she and Gran had had a special relationship. In fact, Gran was the reason why, as a graduate of Boston College's nursing program, Noelle decided to specialize in caring for the elderly. She now headed the health program at an exclusive, assisted-living community outside of Boston. Over the past several years, some of the more active residents had become dear friends. Without them, she would not be in Florida.

Noelle smiled at the memory of Edith Greenbaum confronting her with three of her closest friends at the New Life Assisted-Living Community. "Now you listen here, young lady," Edith had said with great earnestness, "it's time for you to go somewhere, kick up your heels, and have a little fun. I was doing some research on the internet, and I've come up with the right place for you."

Shocked and pleased, Noelle had played along. "And where might that be, boss?"

Edith and the other three women had tittered happily.

"I've printed it out for you." Edith handed her a sheet of information on the Seashell Cottage just south of Clearwater Beach in Florida.

The minute Noelle saw the picture, she knew it was the perfect idea, the perfect place. Sitting on the edge of a broad expanse of white beach, a small, pink cottage beckoned to her.

With its painted clapboards, wide front porch, and two palm trees spreading shade nearby, it was everything she'd imagined in a beach getaway.

"Thank you, Edith," she'd said with meaning. "I'll see if it's at all possible."

"You know we're right, Noelle," Edith replied kindly. "It's time for you to move on with your life. If you don't do it for yourself, at least do it for us. We're stuck here. But you're not."

Tears stung Noelle's eyes as she'd embraced each one. It was the best time of year for her to do as they suggested.

Thinking of those dear women, Noelle's spirits lifted and she began to run.

For the second morning in a row, Noelle awoke and stretched, relieved to be away from home. She'd wanted to come to Florida in time for Thanksgiving, but her mother had put her foot down and insisted she spend Thanksgiving at home with her family. Noelle loved her parents and her three older brothers and their families. But being with them for Thanksgiving had convinced her it was right to come to Florida for the Christmas holidays. Chaos reigned when the whole family was together. Eight nieces and nephews between the ages of one and fourteen were enough to rattle anyone. Even her mother, Jen, went to bed as soon as she could after everyone else had gone, leaving Noelle to do the final cleanup at the end of the evening.

Noelle put on her fuzzy pink robe, padded into the kitchen, and turned on the coffee maker. Through the kitchen window she saw the clouds the weatherman had predicted were marring the blue sky and sometimes hiding the sun. Still, with ice and snow back home, the day seemed full of promise.

She took her cup of coffee out to the front porch and gazed out at the water. A sense of peace washed over her. Edith had told her life was full of challenges, forcing people to grow and change. Thinking of the past two years, she realized she'd been stuck in a pattern of self-doubt and hurt. No man, she vowed, would ever put her through such a humiliating time again. Edith was right. It was time for a change.

With fresh resolve to enjoy each day free from the past, she went inside, changed into shorts and a T-shirt, and headed out to the beach. Though the air was cool, the sun peeked from behind the clouds and felt warm on her face as she headed down the sand at a brisk pace.

Along the shore, snowy egrets were dipping their beaks into the shallow water, retrieving small, silvery fish. Noelle loved their long legs and the dark beaks that accented their white feathers. How long has it been, she wondered, since she'd taken the time to stop and study the beauty around her.

A number of people, children included, were searching the sand at the water's edge for seashells. Some of the more experienced searchers held net bags that sagged with the weight of their treasures. She understood how hooked some people could be on searching for the best and the most unusual shells they could find. Each shell was truly a gift from the sea.

As she got closer to the part of the beach where she'd met Silas, she slowed. But neither Silas nor the dog named Duke were in sight. Sorry to have missed them, she walked on.

When she reached the long, wooden pier that reached out into the water like a finger testing for coldness, she sat down on one of the benches at the end of it. For a while, she watched fishermen patiently waiting for a strike. She especially liked to watch the young boys and girls fishing. The hope on their faces was priceless.

Yawning softly, Noelle headed back to the cottage. The sea air, sun, and freedom from home were working their magic on her body, relaxing muscles that had been tight too long.

In the distance, she could see Silas and his dog playing on the sand. Picking up her speed, she headed toward them.

Duke bounded toward her. His black paws pounded the sand in steady, eager beats. Wagging his tail, he stopped in front of her, tongue hanging out. Laughing, she patted him on the head. "Hello, Duke."

She looked up to see Silas running toward her, waving.

Her heart filled at the sight of him. She'd hoped to have a little boy just like him one day.

"Hi," said Silas, beaming at her. "You're early today."

"Yes, it was such a beautiful morning I decided not to stay in bed. How are you?"

He looked down, kicked at the sand, and looked up at her with a sour expression. "Mrs. Wicked is back."

"Mrs. Wicked?"

He nodded. "She's my Nana's nurse. I don't like her. She's mean. She was on her break. And now the good nurse is gone and Mrs. Wicked is back."

"I see. Well, nursing can be difficult," Noelle ventured to say, unsure what the real problem was in the house.

Silas took hold of her hand. "C'mon! I've got to hurry back.

I'm supposed to stay right in front of Nana's house. If I don't, Mrs. Wicked will be mad."

Noelle allowed herself to be hurried along.

Standing in front of Silas's great-grandmother's house, Noelle studied the old woman.

Even from a small distance, she seemed bowed in spirit and fragile as she sat in her wheelchair staring out at them. Others might not recognize these signs, but from her years of experience with the elderly, Noelle was used to seeing this. On a whim, she turned to Silas.

"Let's go say hello to your grandmother."

"She doesn't talk much," Silas said with a note of sadness in his voice.

Noelle smiled. "That won't matter. I bet she's curious about me and might like a visitor."

As they walked toward the front porch, a figure emerged from the house. Noelle observed the big-boned, broad chested woman and guessed that this was the person Silas called Mrs. Wicked. Her hair was short and dyed a deep black. That and her long, sharp nose made Silas's nickname for her intriguing.

"There she is," whispered Silas.

Pretending not to have heard, Noelle lifted a hand in greeting. "Hello!"

The woman did not return Noelle's greeting and, instead, went inside.

Noelle climbed onto the porch, walked up to Silas's great-grandmother, and held out a hand. "I'm Noelle North, a new friend of Silas's. I thought I'd come say hello to you."

From among the wrinkles and the downcast look on her face, her blue eyes lit and a smile emerged. "I'm Althea. Althea Bellingham." Noelle could see how beautiful the woman must have been and wondered what kind of injuries kept Althea in a wheelchair when there seemed so much life to her.

"She's Mrs. Bellingham to you," said the woman emerging from the house to stand behind Althea. Dressed in dark slacks and a white shirt, she scowled at Silas and turned her disapproval on Noelle.

"And you are?" Noelle asked.

"Betty Wickstrom," the woman said with a challenging expression.

Noelle held back a chuckle. Mrs. Wicked seemed such an appropriate shortened version of the name. She turned to Althea. "Maybe someday Silas and I can get you out in the sun for a bit. He and Duke play a mean game of catch."

Althea nodded and then glanced at Betty.

"She's doing very well right where she is. And now it's time for her medicine. So say goodbye to her."

Althea's expression changed to one of defeat.

"Silas, time for you to come into the house," said Betty.

"No! I don't want to go inside. I want to stay with Noelle."

Noelle smiled at both women. "I'm happy to stay with him for a while longer. Will that be okay?"

"No!" said Betty.

As Althea reached up to touch Betty's arm, her long-sleeved shirt revealed a bruise on her forearm. "Yes."

"What happened to your arm?" Noelle asked as calmly as she could while suspicion rolled through her in a wave of unease.

Althea glanced at Betty.

"She's fine, just a little clumsy, that's all," said Betty, waving away Noelle's concern.

"You hit Nana there," said Silas, moving closer to Noelle. "I saw you."

"Why, you little ... You know that didn't happen. That's where I helped her up from another fall."

Silas clasped Noelle's hand and shook his head. "Adults

aren't supposed to lie."

Noelle knelt down in front of Althea's wheelchair and spoke softly. "Althea, you can trust me. I'm a registered nurse who helps the elderly where I live in New England. Are you being hurt?"

Althea looked at Betty, turned back to Noelle, and nodded. Then she lifted her shirt. Bruises were everywhere.

Noelle scrambled to her feet and faced Betty, her hands fisted. The burning desire to attack the awful woman was almost overwhelming. Through gritted teeth, Noelle said, "I would suggest you pack up your things and leave now, Betty, or I'm calling the authorities."

"You wouldn't dare!" snarled Betty.

"I would, I can, and I will," said Noelle, flexing her fists. The abuse of the elderly wasn't new, but each time she saw an example, it made her sick to her stomach.

Noelle turned to Silas. "You stay here with your great-grandmother. I'm going inside to make sure Mrs. Wickstrom leaves."

Betty placed her hands on her hips and glared at Noelle. "You can't make me leave. You didn't hire me."

"If you don't leave, I'm calling the police to have you removed. I'm not bluffing. I've handled cases like this before," Noelle said, well aware this really wasn't her business. But she wouldn't, she couldn't let the abuse continue. The sight of those bruises felt like a punch to her gut.

"You have no proof that I did anything wrong," countered Betty.

Noelle's smile was cold. "Oh, but I do. I have two very credible witnesses and, if necessary, I'll take photographs to show the authorities. Now, get your things, and I'll escort you to your car."

Noelle followed Betty inside and to a bedroom off the

kitchen in the back of the house. She watched carefully as Betty hastily threw her things into a small suitcase. When she'd zipped her suitcase closed, she turned to Noelle.

"What are you going to do about it now?"

Noelle drew a deep breath. "I'm taking your keys to the house and escorting you to your car."

"And then what?" sneered Betty. "Althea isn't an easy woman to deal with. Too stubborn, too demanding for her own good."

"Come on, let's go."

Noelle escorted Betty outside, wrote down the license number, and stood by as Betty threw her suitcase into the back of a small, blue sedan and climbed behind the wheel. After starting the engine, Betty gave her a middle-finger wave, and took off with a roar.

Alone, Noelle stood in the driveway, breathing in and out in a calming pattern to slow her heartbeat. A sense of dismay made her grow cold. What in the hell had she done? She didn't know Althea Bellingham. And now she was in charge of her until she spoke to her family and they could find other help for her. She went inside the house and out to the seaside porch. Silas was sitting next to the wheelchair, holding his great-grandmother's hand. Althea was asleep in the chair, safely secured. At the sweet sight of them, tears sprang to Noelle's eyes.

"Hello," she said softly to Silas. "Mrs. Wicked is gone. Come with me. I need your help."

Silas followed her into the kitchen.

"Who do I need to call? Where are your parents?" Noelle asked.

Silas gave her a look that was so sad, Noelle's heart clenched. "My dad is in New York. He'll be back at the end of the week."

"Do you have a phone number for him?"

Silas smiled and pointed to a printed list by the kitchen phone. "It's the one on the top. His name is Jake."

Noelle studied the mounted paper. Jake Bellingham's phone number was listed at the top. She picked up the phone and dialed the number.

"The Bellingham Hotel New York. How may I help you today?" came a practiced, professional-sounding voice.

Noelle's heart pounded with dismay. *Bellingham Hotel? The family owned hotels?* "May I please speak to Jake Bellingham?"

"I'll put you through to his office."

After a minute, a feminine voice came on the line. "Mr. Bellingham's office. How may I help you?"

"Please, it's important I speak to him. I'm a visiting neighbor calling from his grandmother's house in Florida about a situation in her home." Noelle's pulse sprinted at the idea of telling him what she'd done.

"Please hold, and I'll see if he can take the call," his secretary said.

A moment later, Noelle heard a deep voice say, "Jake Bellingham."

Noelle swallowed hard. "Mr. Bellingham, you don't know me, but I'm a new friend of Silas's. My name is Noelle North, I'm a registered nurse visiting from Massachusetts, and though I'm not licensed in Florida, I'm calling to tell you that I just escorted your grandmother's caretaker out of the house for abusing her. I specialize in care for the elderly and recognize abuse when I see it. I did not call the police. I need to know what you want me to do next."

"Let me get this straight. You don't know me, my grandmother, or the woman who was taking care of her. Yet you had the balls to throw her out of the house? Is that it?"

"Yes," said Noelle with a confidence she didn't feel. "That's about it. As I said, I am a registered nurse, so I've seen too many cases of abuse like this before. Your grandmother has bruises on her arms and torso that are very telling."

"Abuse? Really? Put Silas on the phone," growled his father.

Noelle handed Silas the phone. "Your father wants to speak to you."

Silas's eyes grew round. He took the phone and listened, then he spoke in a series of staccato sentences. "Yes! I told you Mrs. Wicked was mean! Yes, I like her! Her name is Noelle and she's here on vacation. Nana showed Noelle her bruises. That's why."

After a pause, Silas said, "Love you too, Dad," and handed the phone back to Noelle.

"I had no idea this was happening to my grandmother," said Jake. "I have you to thank for uncovering the situation. I've been mostly away for the last several weeks, and Nana never mentioned any problems with Mrs. Wickstrom. Nor did I notice anything like that. I'm sorry, but it isn't possible for me to make it home for another few days due to some international legal problems. Is there any way you can stay with my grandmother and Silas until I can send someone else to take over for you? In the meantime, who can I call for references on you?"

"You can speak to anyone at the New Life Assisted-Living Community outside of Boston. I handle the health program there. I'm in Florida for a vacation, and as I mentioned earlier, I'm not licensed to practice in Florida, and won't be able to stay with your family for any length of time, and then only as a caretaker, not a nurse."

"Until just this weekend, I promise," said Silas's father. "And if I can find a better service than the one I used for Mrs.

Wickstrom, it could be for only a few hours. Don't worry, I'll pay you well."

Noelle bristled. "You may be used to paying people to do your bidding, but it's not necessary for me. I've done this because I care about your grandmother's health and well-being. Not to get your money."

"Whoa! I didn't mean ... Forget it! I'll be in touch. I appreciate your help."

Noelle hung up the phone, still steaming from the notion that she and her work were for sale when she was just voluntarily helping to resolve a very tough situation.

"You're going to stay with me now?" Silas asked, giving her a wide smile. "Maybe for a long time."

"Just until your father can find a replacement," Noelle said, not wanting to get Silas's hopes up for something that wasn't going to happen. She already knew she didn't like Jake Bellingham.

CHAPTER TWO

While Althea continued to nap on the porch, Noelle went through the house to get acquainted with the layout. She needed to determine how best to handle things. Betty's room behind the kitchen was one of two bedrooms on the first floor with a private bath. Another, larger bedroom faced the Gulf beachfront. An office next to that bedroom completed a separate wing from the main living, dining, and kitchen areas. Upstairs, she discovered four additional bedrooms. The master held a private bathroom, as did one other. The remaining two bedrooms shared a Jack-and-Jill bathroom between them. In one, Legos, Star Wars posters, and other items clearly showed it was Silas's room. As she studied the layout and thought of Althea, an idea came to her. She decided to go ahead with her plan before Jake returned and quickly made a phone call. If she was already in a little trouble with Mr. Jake Bellingham, why not make it big trouble?

An hour later, she and Silas stood by while movers rearranged furniture. No longer would Althea be stuck upstairs, she'd be comfortably settled in the room overlooking the beach and the soothing waves. No more would she be removed from her family; she'd be a big part of it. Research and experience showed that participating in family activities kept patients involved, healthier, and happier.

She interviewed Althea, who told her the injury to her hip was from a fall. No one had overseen a course of proper rehabilitation. Instead, Betty had stuck Althea in a wheelchair where Betty could control her. Noelle also suspected Althea had been given too much medication.

In her wheelchair, Althea watched with interest as her bedroom furniture was brought down to the first-floor bedroom.

"Does this look all right?" Noelle asked her.

A smile creased her face. "Bureau there." Althea pointed to a different wall.

Without hesitation, Noelle directed the movers to change the layout of the room. She'd learned how important it was for each patient to have their space arranged to their liking.

By the time the bedroom was set up, the smile on Althea's face was permanent. Tears glistened in her eyes.

"Thank you," Althea said in a voice gravelly with disuse.

Noelle returned her smile. "I'll see that whoever replaces Betty will be well trained and kind. With any luck, we'll get you out of that wheelchair. I'm not promising you're going to run in any road race, but, hopefully, you won't be as confined as you are. Now, let's take a look outside."

"I'll push Nana's chair," said Silas proudly. "Mrs. Wicked wouldn't let me, but I can do it, Noelle."

"Of course, you can," Noelle said. Interaction with children was another plus for an elderly person. The same with animals. "Where's Duke?"

"Outside," said Silas. "Mrs. Wicked wouldn't let him inside."

"Well, as long as he's well mannered, I see nothing wrong with his being inside." Noelle crossed her fingers, hoping she wasn't going too far with all the changes to the household. But after seeing the bruises on Althea's body, there was no turning back. She'd even oversee hiring someone to take Betty's place. *For free, Jake Bellingham!*

Noelle left Althea and Silas sitting together in Althea's new bedroom and checked the upstairs master bedroom to make sure everything was tidy. The furniture in both rooms was of high quality and tasteful design, so the exchange looked fine. In fact, she liked the upstairs room even better with lighter furniture.

Noelle's stomach growled. She patted it, and realized it was way past lunchtime. A bit worried, she hurried downstairs. She might be a very capable nurse, but she wasn't a great cook. After looking through the cupboards and the refrigerator, she went to Althea's room.

"Silas, what would you like for lunch? A peanut butter and jelly sandwich?"

"Really? I can have one? Mrs. Wicked said peanut butter wasn't good for anyone."

Noelle couldn't hold back a frown. "Althea? Is it okay if Silas has a peanut butter sandwich? No allergies to peanuts?"

"No, I don't have any allergies to peanuts," said Silas. "I know all about it. A boy in my class at school is allergic. We can't have any treats because of it."

"Okay then. You'll have a peanut butter and jelly sandwich. Althea, what can I get for you? Do chicken noodle soup and saltines sound tasty?"

Althea's eyes lit with pleasure. "Nice."

Silas smiled at Noelle. "Nana's talking better now."

"She has a voice now," said Noelle, wondering why no one had seen what was going on with Betty. But then, people like Betty were very clever about hiding things.

Noelle wheeled Althea into the kitchen and settled her at the pine kitchen table while she fixed her soup. Althea may have become silent with despair, but now she chatted away about everything and nothing, mostly stories of the past and the husband she adored.

Noelle and Silas listened quietly as they sat with their sandwiches and Althea finished her soup.

"Are you ready for a nap?" Noelle asked when Althea's head began to nod.

Althea jerked and her eyes flew open. "No pills."

"All right. But I need to know where Betty kept your medications."

"Upstairs in the bathroom," said Silas. "But she kept other ones in her purse. Those are the ones she made Nana take. Something to make her sleep."

"Okay, I'll see to that in a minute. First, we'll get Nana to bed."

After Noelle got Althea to her room, she helped her in the bathroom. Watching the movement of her legs, Noelle's guess that Althea had never received ongoing rehabilitation exercises was confirmed.

Noelle helped Althea onto her bed and pulled a lightweight blanket over her. After Althea was sleeping, Noelle went to the bathroom upstairs to check on the medications. None of the containers of medication contained anything out of the ordinary. Betty had been clever to keep those others out of sight.

Downstairs, Noelle found the phone number of the agency for which Betty had worked and gave them a call. "I'm just reporting the incident," she explained. "I'm sure the family will want to talk to you themselves."

"Thank you," said the manager. "I'm alarmed to hear about this. I assure you we'll investigate the matter right away. Betty Wickstrom is a recent hire to our staff and passed all the requirements and references. Before discussing this with you any further, I'll await a call from a member of the family. You do understand this has to be between us and them for the moment."

"Yes, I do." Satisfied she'd done all she could to resolve the situation, Noelle walked out to the porch. Silas was sitting in a chair, playing a game on his tablet. Duke rose from his spot on the floor next to Silas and came over to greet her. Noelle rubbed the dark fur on his head and sat in a chair beside Silas.

Noelle drew a deep breath and asked the question that had been hovering in her mind like a bee ready to sting. "Silas, did Mrs. Wickstrom ever hurt you?"

"No," he said. "I hid under the bed when she got mad at me."

A shiver traveled down Noelle's back. "How often did that happen?"

"Not many times. I always tried to be quiet around her," he stated in a matter-of-fact way that caused Noelle's heart to skip a beat.

"Did you ever tell your father about any of this?"

Silas shook his head back and forth. "No! I promised her I wouldn't tell anybody so she wouldn't hurt Nana."

Noelle caught her lip, determined not to spill out the anger that was building inside her. She forced herself to say calmly, "Thank you for telling me."

She was about to say more, when a deep voice came from behind her. "So, this is the busybody nurse Jake was talking about."

Noelle jumped to her feet and whirled around. A tall, well-built man with auburn hair faced her. His green eyes raked over her with a sign of interest. Noelle guessed he was in his late thirties, and as handsome a guy as her ex-fiancé.

"Uncle Brett!" cried Silas. He leaped up into his uncle's wide-spread arms. "Noelle saved us from Mrs. Wicked."

Brett's expression grew serious. His eyes sought hers. "Jake called me and I came as quickly as I could. Is it true? Mrs. Wickstrom wasn't doing a good job with Nana?"

"Not only was she not doing a good job, she was abusing your grandmother. It was all cleverly done, hitting or pinching her where others wouldn't see the bruising, hiding medicine in her purse to keep your grandmother sedated and quiet."

The color left Brett's face. He set Silas down on the porch and faced her. "My God! Why didn't we hear about this before now? We've been busy keeping the hotels going, but both Jake and I would've put a stop to it. In fact, if what you're saying is true, I'm reporting her to the police." He studied her. "What is your name again? And how did you get involved with this?"

Noelle couldn't help the flush of color that crept to her cheeks. Blushing had been a betrayer of her emotions all her life. She cleared her throat and stood her ground. "I'm Noelle North, here on vacation. Silas and I have become friends, and that's how I met your grandmother. I'm a registered nurse specializing in the care of the elderly. Back home in New England I run the health program for the New Life Assisted-Living Community outside of Boston. Your brother may think I've intruded, but hopefully you'll understand that once I saw what was taking place, I had to act."

Brett gave her a thoughtful look. He turned to Silas. "Hey, buddy! How about going inside and checking on Nana. I think I hear her voice."

"Okay, but I'm coming right back," said Silas, gazing at his uncle with adoration.

Brett waited until Silas had gone inside and then spoke quietly. "Don't mind Jake. He and I both have a lot on our plates. Our parents' small plane went down somewhere in the Rockies a month ago, and it still hasn't been found."

"Oh, I'm so sorry. That's awful!"

Brett nodded grimly. "It's put the whole family into a tailspin. My mother is the one who looked after Nana and made sure she was well taken care of." He glanced toward the door. "We don't talk about it much in front of Silas because the death of his mother a couple of years ago was so difficult for him. And for Jake, too."

"That's so sad," said Noelle. "I'm truly sorry for all your family is going through. Is Althea aware of this? She talked quite a bit about her husband, Jacob, but never mentioned anyone else."

"I don't know how much Nana really knows about all that's happened. I'm sure you realize she's suffering from Alzheimer's and has good days and bad. We're trying to keep her from worrying. With leaves off the trees now, we're hoping to find my parents' plane. My father has always been active outdoors, but even so, it doesn't look hopeful for them."

Noelle let out the breath she hadn't realized she'd been holding. Like Brett said, things were a mess.

Silas came running onto the porch. "Nana's sleeping. Can I stay with you now, Uncle Brett?"

He ruffled Silas' red locks, so like his own. "Okay, buddy."

Silas tugged on Brett's hand. "Can Noelle stay and be Nana's nurse? She's the best ever!"

"I don't know. That's up to your father. But maybe she'll stay until we get someone new, someone permanent."

Silas' lower lip came out in a pout but he didn't say anything.

Noelle's heart clenched with sympathy. "We can always be friends, Silas, whether I stay here or not."

The satisfaction that brightened his face brought a smile to her. She looked up to see Brett studying her.

"I'll spend the night here, but I have to go back to Miami tomorrow," he said. "Will you stay with Nana and Silas tomorrow and until the weekend when Jake will be here?"

"I'm not registered for nursing care in Florida, so I can't act as Nana's nurse," she told him. "But I'll act as her caretaker until Jake gets here. I'm here only on vacation, so it can't be a long-term thing. And by the way, I took Betty's house keys from her, but you might want to change the locks or security codes on anything else. I wouldn't trust her to stay away."

Looking grim, Brett nodded. "Thanks for everything. Wait until Jake hears more details about what's been going on. He's going to be furious." He gave her a sly look. "Especially when he finds out you've thrown him out of his favorite room here."

"Do you mean Nana's new room?"

"Uh-huh." Brett's smile was more a smirk that sent worry through her. Noelle remembered her brief conversation with Jake Bellingham and knew how difficult he could be.

CHAPTER THREE

A fter Noelle showed Brett where Althea's medicines were kept, she hugged Silas goodbye and patted Duke on the head. Her thoughts were whirling as she left Althea's house and headed to Seashell Cottage.

Nearing the cottage she'd come to love in her short time so far in Florida, Noelle sprinted to it. Small but well-laid out, Seashell Cottage was charming on the outside and newly renovated on the inside, making it a perfect place for a beach vacation.

Noelle climbed the stairs onto the porch, past the hammock chair hanging from a beam in the ceiling over the porch, and unlocked the front door. Stepping inside, she breathed a sigh of relief. What had started out as a peaceful day had turned into an exhausting, emotional one. Even now, she couldn't believe how angry she'd been or how quickly she'd taken control of things without thinking of repercussions. Brett had called her a busybody. The thought of facing Jake gnawed at her insides.

The sun was going down and the air was chilly, but she didn't mind. Sweater weather was fine with her. She changed into warmer clothes and went into the kitchen, where she poured herself a glass of red wine.

Gazing around the interior of the cottage, she thought of how homey it was. It was larger than the word "cottage" implied. Three bedrooms with private baths, a small office, a combined living and dining area, and the kitchen made up the interior. Outside, a screened-in splash pool and patio sat on the south side, and in front, the porch overlooked the beach and Gulf. She thought it was perfect.

Carrying her wine, she went out to the porch and sat down in the swing. The movement of the waves against the wide beach in front of her and the silky taste of the wine slipping down her throat were soothing. She thought about Silas. She'd liked him from their first meeting. But knowing how he bravely did his best to protect his great-grandmother, she understood how very special he was. She couldn't help wondering what his father was like.

She thought about the things she might need at Althea's house and realized until Jake arrived, she'd be there day and night. With her agreement, Brett had cancelled the night help so it would be less confusing for Althea and would feel safer to Silas.

Her cell phone rang. Checking the number, Noelle hesitated. *Her mother.* Aware it would be better to get the call over with, she picked up the call. "Hi, Mom!"

"Hi, darling! How are you doing down there? I must say you picked a great time to head south. The weather is quite miserable here. In fact, if you want company I was thinking I could come down there for a couple of days."

Noelle's heart pounded with dismay. "Thanks anyway. Another time, another place, we can do something together. But I really need this time for myself." Noelle's tongue slipped a little on the lie, but she knew if her mother was aware of what she'd done and had promised to do, she'd be upset. In her mother's world, one would not barge into another's home, order people out, and rearrange their furniture. And on vacation, one would not go to work for someone else, for free or otherwise.

Thankfully, her mother took her at her word. "I understand, darling, I really do. But I miss you so much.

Christmas isn't going to be the same without you. You're my Christmas angel."

"Yes, but maybe it's time for that angel to put away her wings. You know I hate the holidays now."

Her mother let out a long sigh. "From the time you were little, with your blond curls and rosy cheeks, you looked like a cherub. After having three boys, I was thrilled you arrived— my darling little girl, my special Christmas gift."

Noelle told herself not to roll her eyes. This story came up every Christmas. But this year, with all the bad memories, it was too much. She was done with that bit of family history and the holidays. Period.

"Well, I'll go unpack my bags," said her mother.

"Mo-o-o-m!"

"Just kidding," said her mother. "I thought you might want to keep your privacy. Don't worry. I'll find some way for us to do something fun together after the holidays."

"Love you, Mom," Noelle said with feeling. Not every young woman had a mother as warm and wonderful as hers.

"Love you too, honey. Keep in touch."

Noelle clicked off the call and stared out at the water, black now except for the white foam on the edges of the waves striking the sand.

Sighing, she rose and went inside. Tomorrow and for the next two days, she was going to be very busy.

Noelle packed her suitcase and placed it and a canvas catchall bag into her rental car. Gazing at the cottage she'd already grown to love, she reluctantly pulled out of the driveway and headed down the beach to Althea's house. Her vacation was turning into no vacation at all, but it was a situation of her own making and one she didn't regret. Brett had called her early that morning to make sure she was coming.

As she drove into the driveway of Althea's house, Brett was waiting for her outside the house with Silas and Duke. Seeing her, Silas jumped up and down, looking like a kid waiting for a birthday party. Noelle wondered if she'd made a mistake to make such a large commitment to people she barely knew. Then her sense of empathy took over, and she shook off the thought. These were people who needed her.

"Hi, glad you're here," said Brett, rushing over to her to handle her luggage. "I wasn't comfortable trying to get Nana dressed, and now she's upset."

"I'll get her dressed and settled for the day. How about you, Silas? Ready for another nice beach day?"

"Yes! I want you to come swimming with me."

Uncertain how to answer, Noelle glanced at Brett. "Unless I have some relief I won't be able to leave the house."

"Yeah, after you left last night, I thought of that too. Jake has agreed to have me stay until he can get here this weekend and hire new help."

"Okay. That's great. It'll be good for Silas to get out of the house. Right, Silas?"

Silas nodded happily.

Brett ruffled the hair on Silas's head. "I've already promised to take him fishing tomorrow. Today, we'll get all the equipment. What we have here is pretty old stuff."

Silas beamed at them. "I'm going to catch a lot of fish."

Brett and Noelle laughed together.

"I'd better go inside and check on Althea," she said.

Silas took hold of her hand. "I'll help you. She likes me."

Touched by the sweet offer, Noelle allowed him to lead her inside. Duke followed at their heels, with Brett behind carrying her two bags.

"I'm putting you in the master bedroom upstairs," said Brett. "It's more private than the other rooms."

Noelle's eyebrows lifted. "Thanks. That's nice of you."

When Noelle walked into Althea's room, her eyes lit with pleasure. "Hello, Claire."

Silas frowned. "Claire was my mother. She's not here anymore, Nana."

A cloud of confusion dimmed Althea's eyes. "I'm sorry. I thought you were her."

"Noelle doesn't look anything like my mother," Silas said firmly. "She's not like her at all."

Noelle remained quiet. Perhaps, she thought, no one will ever measure up to his mother. According to some of her friends, a son's love was precious. His mother was a lucky woman to have brought up a son like Silas.

For the next hour and twenty minutes, Noelle helped Althea with a shower, gently rubbed skin cream on her dry skin, put a fresh change of clothes on her, and combed her hair. Still horrified by the bruises on Althea's body, Noelle made sure her touches were gentle.

"Thank you, Claire," Althea said with much dignity when they were through with the morning routine.

"Glad to help," said Noelle, unwilling to correct Althea. If, for the moment, she was Claire, it was fine with Noelle.

With Althea prepared for the day, Noelle rolled her wheelchair out to the porch so she could sit in a warm spot and watch the water.

"Wow! Nana looks nice," said Brett. "You sure know your stuff."

Noelle shrugged. "As anyone ages, she should be treated with respect and dignity. And, yes, cleanliness."

Silas joined them. "Nana thinks Noelle is my mother, but she's not."

Brett reached out a hand and patted Silas on the back. "No, she isn't. Noelle's a very nice person who, I bet, would like a cup of coffee and a chance to sit down."

Noelle smiled. "Sounds great."

The three of them went into the kitchen. Noelle helped herself to a cup of coffee and took a seat at the kitchen table.

"I found cereal for breakfast and not much else," said Brett. "Guess someone better go to the store. How are you at grocery shopping?"

"Okay," she said, and clucked her tongue. "It's pretty basic. Have you started a list?"

"No. I thought I'd leave that up to you too."

"Okay, no problem. But I'm curious. You do know how to feed yourself don't you? I mean, buy food, cook it, eat it, clean up afterwards and all?"

He gave her a sheepish grin. "I have a housekeeper who does all that stuff. Growing up, my mother didn't have time to cook. We ate a lot of meals at the hotel."

"Which hotel? You have one in New York and Miami. How many others?"

"We have just one additional hotel. In London. It's fairly new. Jake and I agreed to stop going forward with the one we were going to build in Paris." His face flushed with emotion. "It was a dream of Dad's, but Jake didn't think we should go ahead with it after all that's happened."

Noelle nodded and remained quiet. She'd never met a family quite like theirs.

"Back to grocery shopping," said Brett. "What kind of food do you like?"

"Most anything," she said honestly. "Everyone in my family loves to cook except me. But I love to eat."

His gaze swept over her. "Doesn't look like it."

She swallowed hard and fought the sensual feelings he'd

aroused in her. Warning herself to snap out of it, she said, "Let's just say I enjoy a little bit of delicious food."

He smiled and winked at her. "Me too. Let's get that list going."

They went through cupboards and the refrigerator together, adding anything they could think of. When they were through, Brett handed her a credit card. "Better use this."

Noelle was about to accept the card when Silas came running into the kitchen. "Nana says she needs you, Noelle. I think she's hungry."

"Okay, I'll be right there. Guess you're going grocery shopping, Brett."

The look of surprise on his face was telling. She realized he wasn't used to being given orders and hid a smile. "Unless you'd rather help Nana yourself."

"No, no! I'll go to the store." He turned to Silas. "Want to come with me, buddy?"

"Yes. I'll help you. Dad says you were spoiled as a kid, and you don't know how to do a lot of things."

This time, Noelle couldn't hold back a chuckle. "Kids and the truth, huh?"

He shrugged and grinned. "Can I help it if I was the favorite, spoiled child?"

"No, I am," Silas announced, tapping his chest. "Dad told me I was his favorite person in the whole wide world."

Noelle and Brett exchanged glances.

"Guess you beat everyone else for the title," said Noelle. She didn't dare mention that all three of her brothers accused her of being spoiled. "Now, why don't you two favorite children get going so I can work with Nana."

Brett took a deep breath and let it out. "Jake was right. You sure are bossy."

"I've got three older brothers. I learned early on how best to deal with them," said Noelle, trying not to be stung by his comment.

Brett's eyes twinkled with humor. "See you later, boss lady."

Noelle grinned and shook her head. If Jake was the gruff older brother, Brett was the happy-go-lucky younger one.

Silas surprised her by wrapping his arms around her. "See you later, Noelle."

She gave him a quick hug. "Later, alligator."

As soon as they started for the door, Noelle hurried to Nana.

CHAPTER FOUR

When Althea saw Noelle, she smiled. "You were here yesterday. *You* helped me, not that awful woman."

Noelle took a seat next to Althea's wheelchair and held her hand. "My name is Noelle. Mrs. Wickstrom isn't coming back. I'm here to help you for a few days."

Althea acknowledged that news with a bob of her head. "I'm hungry. Do you have any cookies like my mother used to make for me?"

"Do you remember what they were called?"

"Ginger cookies. My mother was a wonderful baker. I love cookies."

Noelle pulled her cell phone out of her pants pocket and punched in the cell number Brett had given her.

"Yes, boss lady?"

"We need to add ginger cookies to the list. Molasses, too. Althea loves cookies. Thanks!" Noelle clicked off the call before Brett could tease her again. She wasn't that bossy, was she?

Althea stared at the cell phone. "I used to have one of those. But I like the kind that hangs on the wall, like the one I had at my old house."

"Where was that?" Noelle asked, allowing Althea time to drift in the past.

"We lived outside the City, on Long Island. Jacob used to come there on the weekends. The hotel business is very busy he always used to say." Althea closed her eyes.

When Althea remained quiet, Noelle rose to her feet. "I'll

get you a snack now. Lunch will be a few minutes later."

"Ginger cookies. I like cookies."

"I'll do my best, Althea, and then we'd better take care of you."

Althea nodded. "Thank you, Mrs. Bertram. I told Mama you'd help."

Silas sat at the kitchen table eating lunch while Noelle put away the groceries with Brett's help.

"For someone who doesn't know how to cook, you sure know how to organize the kitchen," said Brett, munching on a slice of ham.

"I can cook a little," Noelle admitted. "I just don't like doing it. But I don't mind doing all the rest."

"My Dad is a good cook," said Silas.

Surprised, Noelle glanced at Brett.

He grinned and nodded. "One of Jake's many talents. See why I never bothered to learn beyond the very basics?"

"How much older is Jake than you?" Noelle asked.

"Five years. But don't remind him. He hated turning forty." He straightened. "This has been fun, but I've got to get to work. I'll be using the office here near Nana. Okay with you two?"

"Can Noelle and I go swimming now?" said Silas.

"Sure. If anything comes up with Nana, I'll come get you."

"Yay!" cried Silas. "C'mon, Noelle, let's get changed."

"Okay," said Noelle, smiling when Duke got to his feet and gazed up at her with expectation. "You can come too!"

Duke wagged his tail and trotted toward the porch as Silas tugged Noelle up the stairs.

Inside the master bedroom, Noelle changed into her bathing suit—not the skimpy two piece she'd brought for sunbathing, but a one-piece with sexy cutouts that revealed nothing.

She found where the beach towels were kept and grabbed two.

Silas stood beside her, rocking back and forth on his feet with excitement. Observing him, tenderness filled her for the young boy who seemed so alone. "Let's get sunscreen on you, and then we'll be ready to go."

In the kitchen, Silas showed her where the sunscreen was kept. She helped him rub it onto his fair skin.

"How about you?" Silas said.

"Yes, I need some too."

"Can I help you?" said Brett walking into the room and giving her an appraising look.

Heat filled her cheeks. Noelle knew she wasn't ugly, but she wasn't close to being one of those bathing suit models on the cover of one of the magazines guys seemed to like. The best compliments she got were centered around "cute."

"Hand me the spray can and I'll do your back," Brett said. The grin he gave her was playful.

With no other choice but Silas, she handed it over.

Feeling his hands on her back, she wondered about his love life. He'd made no mention of any other women. In fact, he'd told her almost nothing about his life in Miami, New York, or London.

He patted her on the back. "That part's done. If you want help with any others, I'm here."

She shook her head. "Thanks, but no thanks. I've got it." She turned to find him grinning at her. The kind of sexy grin that caused her to blush again.

Silas tugged on her hand. "Hurry, Noelle. I want to get outside."

Brett looked at Silas. "Okay, I'll leave you two alone."

Intrigued by the way he'd made her feel, Noelle watched Brett until she reminded herself that this vacation was about being nice to herself. That didn't include being attracted to the kind of guy who'd hurt her in the past.

Outside, the sun shone brightly, lightening her mood. The boy and the dog running beside her on the white sand reminded her of summer days in her youth when the family would vacation on Cape Cod. Silas broke into a run toward the water. "Hold on!" She picked up her pace and met him at the water's edge.

The beach in front of Althea's house on this weekday was empty of sunbathers, giving them room to play with the dog. The minute Silas held up the ball in his hand, Duke barked and pranced anxiously for Silas to throw it.

Noelle took a seat on one of the towels. Observing Silas and Duke at play, she wondered what it would be like to have a family of her own. At thirty-two, she felt her biological clock ticking. Yet, she wouldn't, couldn't, rush into anything.

Duke's racing after the ball started to slow down. Noelle checked the time on her phone and was surprised to see how late it was. She called to Silas, and he reluctantly followed her up to the house. Tonight, she was responsible for making dinner and she wanted to make sure it would be a decent one.

After Noelle was dressed and saw that Silas had changed into his clothes, she headed downstairs to check on Althea. When she walked into her room, Althea smiled at her.

"Hello, Noelle."

Surprised and pleased, Noelle responded. "How was your nap? You look refreshed."

"Very nice. That other woman gave me too much medicine."

"I think so," Noelle responded. She'd make sure Jake was aware of that too. Someone like Betty Wickstrom shouldn't be allowed near patients, much less take care of them.

Noelle helped Althea to the bathroom and got her settled in a rocking chair in the living room. "I'd like to see you out of your wheelchair as soon as possible. I'll talk to Brett about getting a physical therapist to help you."

Althea's eyes widened and then filled with tears.

Noelle realized then that Althea's mental issues may have been compounded by too much medication. She turned on a television program and found one that Althea wanted to see and left the room to fetch her a healthy snack.

She passed the office door and turned around. She knocked on the French door and waited for Brett to acknowledge her. He lifted his head, smiled, and waved her inside.

"What's up?"

Noelle told him of her suspicions Althea might not be as mentally impaired as they'd previously thought, that the medications she'd been given had muddled her mind more than usual, and a physical therapist might be able to help Althea move better.

Brett leaned back in his desk chair and gazed at her. "You sure know how to stir things up, but it's all good. I'll make a few calls to find someone to come in. I also have hired a new housekeeper. She'll start on Monday and will watch over Silas too. Over the weekends and on her off days, kitchen cleanup and watching Silas will be part of the nurse's job. Does that sound reasonable?"

"Yes. Make sure Silas is comfortable with both before hiring. If he's to be left here alone, it's important."

Brett frowned. "Jake had no choice but to leave Silas here for his school's winter break. I told him I'd help, and Jake will come to Florida as often as he can. It's the best idea the two of us could come up with. Silas's school has cooperated. His teacher has given him homework and projects for the couple of weeks he'll miss class."

"With all that's happening in your business and with the worry of your parents, it certainly has to be difficult."

Brett looked at her thoughtfully. "Silas loves you. Would you consider being a nanny of sorts? You know, spend several hours a day with him? We'd compensate you well to do it."

Noelle clamped her hands on her hips and glared at him. "What is it with you Bellingham men? I love Silas and had planned to do things on my own with him. And I don't need your money to make me do it. Understand?"

Brett held up his hands to ward off her reply. "Whoa! I didn't see that coming. That's not how people usually respond."

"Well, I can't help how I feel." Noelle turned and left the office. *People with money sometimes thought they owned the world. Well, they don't own me!*

Dinner that night turned out to be one of Noelle's better attempts—a chicken casserole that her mother liked to make. It was super easy and downright delicious. Maybe because it was one of the first things she'd learned to make back when she had the time to fuss over meals for herself.

She was pleased when Brett asked for seconds. And when Silas declared it was the best meal he'd ever eaten, she was thrilled by the praise. Maybe cooking wasn't as bad as she'd thought.

Later, when she was preparing to go up to her room to read, Silas hurried over to her. "Will you read me a story?"

"Of course. Why don't you brush your teeth and get in your pajamas, and then I'll come to your room? Pick one of your favorite books."

"A big, thick book?" Silas shot her a mischievous look.

"If it's a really long story, we'll read a couple of chapters each night until it's time for me to leave."

"Leave? But I don't want you to leave. I want you to stay here," Silas said. His lower lip jutted out quivering a bit.

Noelle put an arm around him. "We're friends, right?"

He gazed at her and nodded.

She smiled down at him. "We can be friends here or elsewhere. Don't worry, we'll work things out."

His green eyes settled on her with hope.

She hugged him, wondering how this little boy had wheedled his way into her heart so quickly.

Upstairs, Noelle sat in a chair next to Silas's bed, reading aloud a story about a boy named Harry. Silas listened intently and then his eyes began to close. Noelle closed the book and quietly rose to her feet.

Silas's eyelids fluttered. Then he opened his eyes. "Noelle? Do you believe in Christmas magic?"

Taken aback, Noelle said, "I used to. Why?"

"My mother loved Christmas the best of all. Will you help me decorate a tree for Christmas? Dad and I haven't had a Christmas tree since Mom died." The pleading in his voice and the beseeching look on his face made her uncomfortable. This was her time to be free of Christmas and all the memories of the one that had gone bad.

"We'll talk about it tomorrow," said Noelle. Maybe by then she'd come up with a reasonable excuse to bow out of it gracefully.

"Okay," Silas said with resignation. Noelle knew by the sound of his voice and the way his shoulders slumped that he missed doing a lot of things he'd done in the past. Was Jake Bellingham so busy, so unfeeling he couldn't see what his son needed?

Noelle bent over and kissed the top of Silas's head. "Good

night. See you tomorrow."

"No! Say that thing about the 'gator," said Silas.

"Oh, okay. See you later, alligator."

Silas smiled and rolled over in his bed.

Later, lying in the large bed in the master suite, Noelle stared up at the ceiling fan whirling slowly above her. Being with Silas and his family had turned what should have been a vacation into a bucket-load of worries. And it was all her doing.

Noelle awoke to gray skies and a stiff Gulf breeze off the water. *A perfect day to stay inside,"* she thought, climbing out of bed. She put on a robe and ran a brush through her blond curls, bemoaning the way the salt air had formed them tighter. Wondering how Althea had fared in the night, she hurried downstairs.

At the bottom of the stairway she heard deep voices in the kitchen and went to investigate.

"Here she is," said Brett. He was wearing jeans, a T-shirt, and a smug smile.

The man next to him was dressed in tan slacks and a button-down shirt that looked newly pressed. He was taller and broader than Brett—an imposing figure. His dark-brown hair held a touch of red and was slicked back above chiseled, classic features. Steely-gray eyes settled on her with a steady, cool stare.

Straightening, doing her best to seem professional while in her pajamas, she held out her hand. "You must be Silas's father. Glad to meet you, Mr. Bellingham."

He gripped her hand. "Ah, I get to meet the bossy nurse at last. It's been what? Three days? And you've changed everything around. I went to climb into my bed late last night only to discover my bedroom is now upstairs, and it isn't the master suite."

"I put her there," said Brett coming to her defense. "But the other stuff is on her." He winked at her.

Noelle pressed her lips together. His actions were something one of her brothers would do—help her out and then shove her under the bus.

"I need to talk to you about a lot of things," said Noelle, striving to be businesslike, while her hand burned in his.

"I bet you do," said Jake, studying her with an expression that wasn't all that friendly.

Noelle swallowed hard and then spoke in what she hoped was a strong voice. "Before we talk, I need to check on Althea. I'll be right back."

The surprise on Jake's face was almost comical. Clearly, no one got away with telling him anything.

Noelle hurried out of the room before he could call her back.

CHAPTER FIVE

When Noelle returned to the kitchen some forty minutes later, Jake was sitting at the kitchen table with Silas. Still in her robe, she realized it was not a suitable appearance for a business discussion, but what choice did she have?

"I'm sorry it's taken so long," she told Jake, "but Althea wanted to get dressed and now I have to take breakfast to her."

Silas leaped off his chair and rushed over to her. "Hi, Noelle. Dad's here. I told him I want you to be my new mother."

Noelle's jaw dropped. It took her a few seconds to recover. "Silas, honey, I'm just a visitor here on vacation for a few weeks."

"I know," said Silas, giving her a warm smile and hugging her around the waist.

Noelle gave Jake a helpless look.

"Silas, enough. Come finish your breakfast," Jake said in a commanding voice that made Silas drop his arms and turn away from her.

Silent, still shaken, Noelle began to put together a simple breakfast for Althea.

Jake cleared his throat. "Why don't we meet in, say, twenty minutes in my office? We'll have more privacy there."

"Me, too, Dad!" cried Silas.

"As soon as Noelle and I are through with our talk, you and I will have time for a talk of our own."

"Okaaay," said Silas. "Then can we play a game together? I've learned a new one."

"We'll see, buddy. I have work to do."

Disappointment washed over Silas's face, but he nodded. Noelle was sure Silas heard this a lot, and her heart went out to him.

After Althea finished her meal another forty minutes later, Noelle raced into the shower and dressed quickly. She told herself it didn't really matter what she looked like, she was merely the help. But that didn't stop her from taking extra care with her hair or putting on lipstick in a warm coral shade.

When she walked into the office, Jake eyed her and nodded. "That's better. Now, let's get to that talk. Brett and I discussed the changes in the room arrangements and we agree that it's much nicer for Nana to be on the ground floor. I understand he's also hired a housekeeper. What we need to do now is hire a nurse or two. By the way, I checked your credentials, and I must say, they're impressive. But Brett informed me that you are not interested in a job here, that you're in Florida for a vacation as you told me."

"Right. And when a new caretaker is hired, you will make sure it's with Silas's approval, won't you?"

Jake frowned at her. "His approval?"

Noelle hesitated for just a second or two. "This isn't a great place for a young child alone, with no active family members around. He'll want to be comfortable with the staff, especially after dealing with Mrs. Wickstrom. Are you aware he had to hide under the bed to avoid her bad temper?"

The color drained from Jake's face. "No, I'm not. Why didn't Silas tell me about what was really happening at here?"

"I suspect Betty Wickstrom took care to see that you weren't told. She threatened Silas with harm to Nana if he told you."

Jake slapped a hand down on the desk. "That's unacceptable! I'm filing charges against her and the agency. And I'll have a talk with Silas too."

"Good. Silas is a wonderful little boy. He's really touched me in the short time we've known one another."

"He misses his mother, I know." He gave her a steady look. "But I have no intention of marrying again."

"I'm sorry about all that's happened to your family. I understand your parents are missing in dangerous conditions."

Jake stared through the window at the greenery outside. When he faced her again, the sadness etched on his features was heartbreaking.

"I think you ought to know that after you get a housekeeper and nurses on board, I intend to see Silas now and then. It has nothing to do with what your brother offered me. I turned him down flat. I don't want your money."

Jake's look held interest as he gazed at her. "You sure are a prickly, bossy little thing."

Noelle decided to let his name calling go unanswered. He was a man under tremendous pressure, and so far, he'd been kinder than she'd thought he'd be.

"Silas tells me you're going to help him celebrate by decorating a Christmas tree this year. Since Claire died, we haven't done much to celebrate the season, other than exchanging gifts. My parents decorated their house, but Silas and I didn't bother with ours."

A battle took place inside Noelle. She wanted to help Silas, but she disliked the idea of being part of a holiday she was trying to forget.

"Isn't that so?" Jake asked her.

She tried for a casual response. "I'm not celebrating Christmas this year. A lot of bad memories."

His eyes seemed to reach inside to the part of her that was quaking. *Please,* she thought, *don't ask any questions about it.*

"That's odd. I would've taken you for the sort that would go all out for Christmas."

Noelle didn't know if that was a compliment or not.

"Well, now that you've more or less placed yourself in the household, I'm asking you to help Silas out. He's been struggling with a lot of things lately—adjusting to life without his mother, then my parents' plane crash. These are life issues even adults would have trouble coping with. Perhaps having Christmas become a true holiday will make things easier for him." His mouth twisted with distaste. "My wife used to love this time of year."

They stared at one another for a few seconds in a silent agreement not to ask further questions. Each obviously had a history they were not about to share.

"Is everything settled now?" Jake asked. "I've been informed that you would like to interview prospective nurses. I'll observe but leave that in your hands." He rose, signaling an end to the meeting.

Noelle got to her feet wishing she'd had a chance to have a cup of coffee before talking with him. Her tattered nerves needed a big boost of caffeine.

Noelle was straightening Althea's room when Brett walked in. "Guess you and Jake got everything straightened out, huh?"

She shrugged. "I guess. I'll interview the candidates for new nurses and hang out with Silas now and then."

"Yeah, he's real excited about Christmas this year."

Noelle held back a groan. She'd wanted to talk to Silas

about maybe doing other things, but now it was out of the question. Everyone seemed to think she'd do this for Silas. And ... well ... she guessed she would. She couldn't let him down. Especially now that she knew there was another story behind Christmases past. From the look on Jake's face, they hadn't been that great except for his son.

"Now that Jake is here, I'm going to pack up and leave," said Noelle. "We should be able to find a suitable nurse if only for a temporary time. Jake has lined up two interviews for this afternoon."

Brett cocked an eyebrow at her. "You're giving Jake the master suite?"

"Yes. My being in that room was all your fault, something you did to annoy your brother. Did you always fight as kids?"

The smile on Brett's face left. "Jake was a very good big brother to me, not always willing to get into trouble. But when I needed him, he stood by me.

Remembering how her brothers acted, she understood. Josh, her oldest brother, was the serious one. Rick, two years younger, was the typical middle child, and Mike, the youngest, was a clown seeking attention from his brothers and trying to take attention away from her.

"Hey, look," said Brett. "I know I've been teasing you a lot. Truth is, I've never met anyone quite like you. I feel as if I've known you a long time."

She placed her hands on her hips. "Is that one of your standard lines?"

Brett held up his hands and backed away. "No, I promise. Not this time."

She studied him. "I would think someone like you wouldn't need a line like that. I bet you have girlfriends in every city."

His grin was sheepish. "Just two."

Noelle shook her head. The Bellingham brothers were

dangerous in so many ways. Vowing to be careful, she left him to go upstairs and pack.

As she was packing, Silas came into her room.

"Dad says you're moving out, but will come and see me every day. Right, Noelle?"

She set down the sweater she'd just picked up and turned to him. "Yes, I will. And if you like, I'll show you Seashell Cottage, where I'm staying. You'll see it's not far from here."

"Are you leaving now?"

"I'm just taking my things back to the cottage and then returning. Your father and I are going to interview nurses to help your Nana."

"Oh, okay." Silas kicked at the carpet with a sneaker and then gazed up at her. "Dad told me not to tell you, but he really likes that you're in charge."

Noelle's eyes widened with surprise. "He does, does he?"

"Not all the time," Silas quickly said. "Just with the nurses."

"Oh, that sounds more like it," said Noelle.

Silas nodded emphatically, bringing a chuckle to her throat.

The first nurse she and Jake interviewed was very competent but with no personality. When Silas was brought in to say hello, she almost recoiled. And that was that.

The second nurse held more promise. Short and round-bodied, her pleasant face lit with tenderness as, with an easy laugh, Dora Williams talked about her grandchildren. A widow now and tired of the shifts at the various hospitals, Dora had decided to do private nursing. The only problem was she wouldn't spend more than four nights a week away from her home. But her credentials and references were perfect. And when Silas immediately went to her for a hug as Dora suggested, Noelle and Jake exchanged hopeful glances.

Jake rose to his feet. "Dora, if you don't mind waiting here a minute, Noelle and I will discuss your candidacy in private and return to you shortly," said Jake, signaling Noelle to follow him out of the room.

Dora nodded and smiled. "You go right ahead. Silas and I will get acquainted."

In the kitchen, Jake turned to Noelle. "What do you think?"

"She's perfect for the job. But now you'll have to find a night nurse."

His gray eyes filled with pleading. "Would you be willing to cover for the three nights Dora can't be here this next week or until we find someone to fill those spots?"

Noelle gazed at her surroundings and wondered if she'd made a huge mistake by being caught up in this family. Then she heard Edith Greenbaum's voice in her head. *Move on with your life. If you don't do it for yourself, at least do it for us. We're stuck here. But you're not."*

"All right. I'll do it," Noelle said. "But I don't know how much more help I can give. I'm here just until the middle of January. Then I need to get back to my life in Boston."

"Okay. That's a deal." Jake held out his hand, and Noelle took it, admiring the silvery gleam of pleasure in Jake's eyes. It had almost been worth it to agree to do the work just to see the change in them.

When they returned to the office, Dora and Silas were chatting happily.

"All right, Dora," said Jake. "I think we have a plan we can all work with thanks to Noelle's agreement to fill in until we find more help. Silas, will you go get Uncle Brett, so he can meet Dora?"

After Silas left the room, they quickly agreed on a schedule and payment for Dora.

Smiling broadly, Dora stood. "Okay, when do you want me to start?"

Noelle and Jake exchanged glances.

"How about now?" Noelle said. "I'll show you to the small suite that will be yours, here on the first floor."

As Noelle led Dora out of the room, Noelle turned back.

Jake was studying her with a thoughtful expression.

CHAPTER SIX

Noelle walked into Seashell Cottage, plunked down her suitcase and canvas carrying bag, and let out a long sigh of happiness. She was back in her own space again. It felt wonderful.

As she placed her things in the bureau of the room she was using, she realized it might be a smart idea to set up an emergency bag of items she'd need if she was unexpectedly called to help the Bellinghams. At first, the thought of living in two places was unsettling, but being at Seashell Cottage already meant she was living like a traveler.

Noelle poured herself a glass of wine. Brett had asked her to stay for dinner, but Noelle had opted to come home to the cottage. Dora, it turned out, was a fabulous cook, and Noelle wasn't needed.

The wind had died down, and the setting sun sent enticing colors through and around the clouds at the horizon, like a rainbow playing hide and seek. Bundling up, Noelle took her glass of wine out to the front porch. She needed the peace of the water's movement and the swirling cries of the birds to settle her thoughts.

The Bellingham brothers were handsome and rich, well-traveled, sophisticated—everything she wanted to avoid in any new relationship with a man. *Been there once*, she thought. She tried to control the acid rushing into her stomach. Alexander Cabot had been just like them— handsome, rich, and polished. And, it turned out, unfaithful. Even now she wanted to shout and scream at the cruelty of his leaving her at the altar for an old girlfriend, the wife of one of his friends. Social media had had a field day with the news, making her seem like a social climbing gold digger—someone Alex was lucky to escape. Especially to those in his social circles, people with money and power. The gossipy news was picked up by people in other states and had even made a blurb in one of the popular, lurid, national magazines.

The trouble, she thought, *was that people like Alex and the Bellingham brothers had the means to satisfy their every whim, making them totally selfish.*

Her thoughts turned to Silas. He was a dear little boy—eager to be friends and to be loved. The thought of his hiding from Betty Wickstrom made her nauseous. If, during her short vacation she could make a positive difference in his life, she'd try. She still didn't like the idea of being thrust into preparations for Christmas, but she'd think of something that might help them both.

The next morning, Noelle awoke with a headache. She went to the window and looked outside. Gray clouds scuttled across the sky, moved along by the wind that had kicked up in a stiff, onshore breeze. *Another good day to stay inside and lay low,* she thought. Barefoot and still in her pajamas, she padded into the kitchen for a cup of hot tea.

She'd had such terrible dreams in the night—dreams of her wedding day mixed with a bizarre chase through a hotel by a black dog that was really a black bear that morphed into a spider. Even now, the thought of that giant spider sent her stomach whirling.

She took a seat at the kitchen table with a sigh. *Why did things have to be difficult?* She should have kept on walking when she saw Silas playing with his dog. But she knew she'd done the right thing by getting rid of Betty Wickstrom, even if it was out of line for a stranger to do it. And then she had no choice but to see the situation through.

She'd just put butter and some blueberry jam on a piece of toast when her cell phone rang. She checked caller ID and smiled. *Edith Greenbaum.* Of all the women she was close to at New Life, Edith was the person she most loved. Some thought of Edith as being too brusque, too outspoken, but Noelle adored that about her. They could talk about real issues openly. Noelle learned that Edith, like others in the community, had no one to assist her through the process of aging and had agreed to help her in any way necessary.

"Good morning, Edith. How are you?" Noelle said, making her voice sound upbeat. Edith was in her late seventies. Her husband and only son had both died, leaving her with money, but no other family.

"We miss you here in Boston," said Edith. "We're calling to see how you are. Hazel has put you on speaker phone."

"Hello, everyone!" Noelle said.

A quartet of replies answered her.

"It hasn't been long we know," said Rose Ragazzi, "but Dorothy had a dream about you meeting some man, and we decided to call you together." Rose had just turned seventy-two and was the most physically active of the group. Unwilling to live with any of her three daughters and sons-in-law, she'd secretly made arrangements to move into the New Life community before anyone could stop her. With her short, gray hair, dark, intelligent eyes, and trim body, she looked more like sixty as she jogged through the complex in the yoga pants she loved to wear.

Noelle knew they couldn't see her, but she wagged a finger in the air. "You know miracles don't happen overnight. I'm not likely to meet any man I'd be willing to date. I haven't so far."

"You will. I'm sure of it. Just remember to enjoy every moment you can," said Dorothy Adams. "And if he looks like the man in my dream, you're in for a nice time." Dorothy, in her early eighties and the oldest of the group, had been widowed at an early age. Of medium height and size, she dressed provocatively young for her age, colored her hair, and carefully applied makeup every morning. Noelle loved her flamboyance. Dorothy's only child, a son, lived nearby but was busy with his own insurance company and didn't spend much time with her. Dorothy loved gossip and news about movie stars and talked about them like they were family. She, more than the others, was determined that Noelle find a decent, handsome man.

"When you least expect it, you'll find someone. A pretty, young girl like you isn't meant to be alone," added Hazel Vogel. Hazel was a prim seventy-four and was easily offended by bad language or bad manners. The only one of them who had never married, she talked of her nieces and nephews as if they were her own, though they'd all moved away from Boston and seldom saw her. Sweet in nature, she was the worrier of the group, keeping track of everyone.

"If something exciting happens," said Noelle, "I'll be certain to let you all know. How's everyone up there?"

"Same old thing," said Edith. "The young waitress we all liked has left and the new one seems to be lazy. But the chef made a delicious meal last night, so we're all happy about that."

"How about the bridge competition. Are the four of you still in the lead?"

"Oh, yes," said Edith with a note of pride. "I don't think any other foursome can beat us."

Noelle smiled. "The Three Musketeers Plus One" they sometimes called themselves.

"I'm glad to hear things are going well up there. I'd better let you go. It's time for your morning coffee meeting. Thanks for calling. I'm sending each and every one of you a big hug from me."

"And back to you!"

"'Bye, honey!

"Have a nice day, Noelle!"

"Talk to you soon, I hope!"

Smiling, Noelle clicked off the call. Edith and her cohorts had buoyed her spirits over and over again. She'd be forever grateful to them.

As if by magic, a ray of sun broke through the clouds, a sign of good things to come. Noelle took a deep breath and decided to take a walk along the beach. She was feeling better already. No more would she take on any unnecessary burdens, she vowed. This was her vacation. She'd see Silas now and then as she'd promised. The rest of the time she'd totally relax—something she seldom ever allowed herself.

Dressed in a light-blue sweater, blue jeans and sneakers, Noelle pulled on a pink windbreaker and went outside. Instead of going south along the beach past Althea's house, Noelle headed north.

The tang of the salty air filled her lungs and soothed her mind. It was all good, she decided. She'd wanted a different kind of holiday season, and she was getting it. She noticed a shell riding the edge of a wave that had just landed on shore and hurried to pick it up.

A tulip shell, she thought, pulling her small book on shells from her jacket pocket. She stood a moment to study the photographs inside the book and confirmed that it was a tulip shell. A nice one. She carefully placed the shell in one pocket of her jacket and the book in another.

Suddenly she knew exactly how to solve the problem of a

Christmas tree for Silas. Satisfied with her plan, she headed south.

She heard the sound of feet slapping the sand behind her and turned to see Brett running along the beach in running shorts and a tank top.

When he realized who she was, he slowed and stopped. "What are you doing out here on this windy day?"

She smiled. "'Thought some fresh air might do me good."

He studied her. "Your cheeks are all pink."

She couldn't stop herself from brushing at her cheeks with her fingertips. Her mother had the same sensitive skin.

"It's all right. It's cute," Brett said, gazing at her with interest. "I understand you and Silas are going to decorate a Christmas tree at Nana's house. Thanks for doing that. Neither Jake nor I have the time or inclination to take care of it. But Silas needs his Christmas. I get that."

"As a matter of fact, I've come up with an idea he and I can work on together. Something different."

"Jake told me you didn't want to celebrate the holidays this year. What's up with that?"

Noelle shrugged. "A sad story. Nothing more."

"So, what's your Christmas idea with Silas?" said Brett, thankfully not pursuing her comment.

She grinned at him. "That's going to be our surprise. No peeking, either."

He held up his hands. "Deal. By the way, I'm going back to Miami this morning and then I'll head to New York and London. Jake will be working at Nana's for most of the month."

"Really?"

Brett nodded. "Yeah. Jake felt terrible about the treatment of Nana and Silas by Mrs. Wicked, as Silas called her. Hope you don't mind having him there. Jake can sometimes be tough to deal with, but after all that's happened to him, who could blame him for being that way?"

"You mean all that's happened with your mother and father?"

Brett shook his head. "No, it's more than that. It's all the problems with Claire." He stopped talking and took a deep breath. "Hey, look! You never heard anything from me. Got it?"

"Okay," Noelle said, wondering what he couldn't say to her.

"If you're headed to Nana's house, I'll walk you there. I've had a great run."

"Thanks. I want to talk to Silas."

Aside from a brief comment on the weather, there was no talk between them as they walked along. But it was a comfortable silence for two people who didn't really know each other.

From the corner of her eye, Noelle studied Brett. Though Jakes' features were sharper, they bore a strong resemblance. Each handsome man carried himself well, with authority. Noelle both liked and was put off by the self-confidence that came from living in their high-powered worlds.

In the distance, they could see Silas playing with Duke.

"Silas sure loves that dog," commented Brett.

"They're really good together. It must be lonely for Silas with his father and you gone. Dora is going to be a very nice addition to the household, don't you think?"

"Yeah. She's a great cook too!" He patted his flat stomach. "Gotta love an older woman who knows how to cook."

Hearing the teasing note in his voice, Noelle laughed. "You're awful. Seriously? You have two girlfriends?"

The smile left Brett's face. He shook his head. "The last one dumped me. Told me I was never around. That's the bad part of the hotel business. It's 24/7."

Duke bounded toward them, barking happily.

"Noelle!" shouted Silas, running toward her on sturdy legs. She smiled and held out her arms to him.

Silas ran into her embrace and clung to her. "I thought ... I thought you weren't coming back." Tears glistened in his eyes.

Noelle got down on her knees and held him tight to her chest. "Listen, Silas. I can't always be with you, but I would never leave without saying goodbye." She looked up at Brett, suddenly understanding that this is what had happened with Silas's mother.

She steadied Silas on his feet and rose. "I've got some pretty interesting plans for the holiday decorations. I think you're going to like them, especially because it'll be our secret."

Silas's face brightened. "A secret? Really? Cool."

Behind Silas, Brett gave her a smile that warmed her heart. Silas might be a boy left at home with others a lot of the time, but there was no doubt that both his father and his uncle loved him.

"Guess I'd better head on home by myself," said Brett. "Sounds like the two of you have a lot to talk about, and I wouldn't want to ruin your secret."

"Please tell Jake that we'll be back there in a while. We're going to take a walk along the beach." Noelle placed a hand on Silas's shoulder and they walked away.

Silas all but danced at her feet. "What's the secret?"

Noelle gazed at the excitement on his face and hoped she wasn't wrong about this. "You know how you wanted to do something special for the holiday season? I've come up with an idea for a very different kind of Christmas tree. How would you like to have a seashell tree?"

Silas looked at her and frowned. "A tree made of seashells?"

Her lips curved. "No, a real, live Christmas tree decorated

with seashells and other treasures from the beach."

His eyes lit with excitement. "Cool. Things we find together. Right?"

"Yes. Every day together we'll collect shells. Then, at Seashell Cottage, where I'm staying, we'll glue ribbons or strings to them to hang on the tree. How does that sound?"

"Cool. Very cool." Silas ran ahead of her, his face turned to the ground.

"Hold on," said Noelle. "Looking for seashells is a very careful business. It takes time to find a nice one." She pulled the tulip shell out of her pocket and gave it to him. "This is a tulip shell." She handed him the small book about shells. "Look in here. We'll learn about a lot of different shells together."

He leafed through the book. "I know I've seen some of these before."

"I'm sure you have. We've got time to find suitable ones. So, no need to hurry."

"But I want lots of them," said Silas.

She smiled and ruffled his hair. "Me too." A warm feeling filled her. She knew working together on this project was the right thing to do. Celebrating with a little boy who needed her wouldn't be a reminder of Christmases past. It was a new beginning. And maybe this would allow her truly to move on.

They spent some time searching for shells. Each time one appeared unusual, they looked it up in the book. After a while, with several shells stowed in her jacket pocket, they headed back to Althea's house.

"I'll get some ribbon and a glue gun so we can make ornaments out of the shells. With permission from your father, you can go with me. Let's go ask him now."

Silas ran ahead of her. She let him go. Observing his legs moving as fast as they could, she was touched by his response to her suggestions. She wondered what it would be like to have a little boy of her own, maybe several. And she'd always wanted daughters. A whole houseful of children. Sadness tugged at her heart and slowed her steps. Those days were still a dream.

When Noelle knocked on the door, Dora answered it and stepped outside onto the porch. "Noelle, I'm so glad to see you. Silas was very upset earlier when he thought you weren't coming to see him today. That boy sure does love you."

"Yes, we've made a wonderful connection. I want him to understand, though, that I'm here only temporarily. I will be returning to Boston two weeks after the New Year."

"I see. Well, in the meantime, it's wonderful of you to take such an interest in him. I know how much it means to him." Her smile was warm as she patted Noelle on the back. "Thanks for helping me to get this job. It's going to be a nice one for me."

"Brett is already admiring your cooking."

Dora laughed. "That man can eat a lot. But by the looks of him, he runs off any fat. In my day, we'd call him a hunk. Now I guess people say 'he's a hottie!'"

Noelle and Dora exchanged smiles and then went inside.

Noelle found Jake is his office, Silas at his side.

He waved her inside. "Silas tells me you've got a big secret for Christmas."

"Yes. We've come up with a plan for your Christmas tree."

He nodded and turned to Silas. "Run along to the kitchen and ask Dora for a morning snack. I need to talk to Noelle alone."

After Silas left the office, Jake got up and closed the door.

"Please sit," he said.

Noelle gave him a questioning look but did as he'd asked.

Jake's gaze settled on her, making her shift in her chair. "It's wonderful that you've taken such an interest in Silas," he said, "but I'm concerned about it going too far. He obviously adores you, but that might only hurt him in the end."

"I'm concerned, too. He apparently panicked when he thought I wasn't coming back. I gather that was something that happened with his mother."

Jake's expression was more than sad; it was one of hurt too. "She dropped dead of a brain aneurysm, so naturally Silas had no chance to say goodbye. It was very hard on him."

"I see," said Noelle wondering why he hadn't said it was hard on both of them.

"Silas mentioned going to Seashell Cottage, the house where you're staying, to help you with the decorations. Is that correct?"

"Yes, I was going to ask your permission for him to spend some time there alone with me from time to time. Also, I told him I'd ask your permission for him to accompany me to a store to buy some supplies for the decorations."

Jake arched his eyebrows. "You're not going to buy the decorations. I'll be glad to pay for anything you need."

Noelle shook her head. "Thanks, but it won't cost much. But if you wouldn't mind buying a small Christmas tree, that would be perfect. We won't decorate it until later, but with it here you'd at least have the smell of evergreens in the house, and I'd know how many decorations we'd need." Jake's expression was full of humor. "And I assume you'd want to come along and make sure I picked the right one?

The dreaded pink from a blush colored her cheeks. "Only if you insisted."

He laughed, spreading light to those gray eyes of his. "I think probably Silas and I will insist on it. I know he'd be disappointed if you didn't come with us."

And you? Noelle silently asked, and wondered why she even cared.

Jake checked his watch. "My call to London can wait until later. Why don't we go get a tree now? I noticed some for sale not far from here, and it's important to get one in water as soon as possible. Most of the trees are shipped down here from North Carolina and other states north of us."

When Silas heard the news, he took hold of Noelle's hand and led her outside to the black Range Rover sitting in the driveway.

CHAPTER SEVEN

In the parking lot of a nearby neighborhood mall, Noelle stood with Jake watching Silas run from one tree mounted on a stand to another, proclaiming each one perfect. She'd forgotten how joyful searching for the right tree could be.

"Do you think we're going to find the perfect one?" Jake asked.

"It might take a while," Noelle responded, smiling at him.

He studied her for a moment and then said, "I have a proposition for you."

She stepped back. "You're propositioning me?"

"What? No. What I meant to say is that I was talking to Dora about Silas, and she had a suggestion that made sense to me. She thought it might be helpful to Silas if he saw the hotel in Miami and my office there. It would help him understand why I'm away so often."

"And?"

"And she suggested it might be useful if you went along to keep an eye on Silas." His lips curved. "You could call it an adventure."

"What length of time are we talking about? Going over in the morning and coming back in the afternoon?"

"Actually, I was thinking of going over this afternoon and returning sometime tomorrow."

"So, I'd be your nanny for the day. Is that it?"

The look on his face was sheepish. "I didn't mean it like that. We'd all go to dinner together but then, yes, you'd stay with him while I attended to some business in the hotel."

Noelle turned away from him, so conflicted she couldn't speak for a moment. It would be fun to visit the hotel, but she was being put in an awkward situation again. She observed Silas standing by a tree he thought was perfect, and she knew she wouldn't turn down the invitation.

She turned back to Jake. "I'll do it, but if you so much as even mention money, the deal's off."

Jake shook his head. "I don't know what it is about you and money, but okay, I won't mention it."

Noelle nodded her agreement. She wasn't about to explain to Jake that Alex thought his money could buy her and anyone else. As it turned out, his money did work in his favor when he wooed and won the love of his struggling friend's wife. The hurt and humiliation caused by his actions were something she'd never forget.

After Jake and Silas had finally agreed on a tree and loaded it onto the roof rack of the Range Rover, they headed back to Althea's house.

"Why don't I drop you off at Seashell Cottage. Okay?" said Jake. Silas and I will pick you up at one."

"Where are we going?" Silas asked.

"On an adventure," Jake answered, winking at his son.

"Noelle is coming too?" At the nod of his father's head, Silas announced. "I like adventures."

Noelle and Jake laughed softly. Maybe, thought Noelle, this will be a pleasant excursion, after all.

Back at Seashell Cottage, Noelle looked through the clothes hanging in her closet. When she'd been dating Alex, her wardrobe had been full of the high-end clothing their socializing had required. Now, with her work centered around the New Life Assisted-Living Community and her social life all but nonexistent, her choice of vacation clothing was limited. She had brought two dresses, though, and quickly chose the black, sleeveless cocktail dress she loved. Aside from that, her daytime clothing would do. After all, he might have disagreed, but basically her job of this trip was that of nanny.

She wondered if Jake's appointments at the hotel included seeing a woman friend, but quickly dismissed that thought as none of her business. If she wanted to date someone in a position of power and prestige, he would be an easy choice. But, once burned, twice shy, as the saying went.

When Jake drove into the driveway of the cottage, she was packed and ready. She hadn't been to Miami in years. Three, in fact. And then it had been simply a stop before taking a private cruise in the Caribbean. She'd looked up The Bellingham Miami hotel and found it was located in South Beach. In that atmosphere of sex, drugs, and rock and roll, it was no wonder Jake wanted Silas to have a steadfast guardian at his side.

Jake loaded her suitcase into the back of the car. "Packing light?"

She nodded. "No reason to do otherwise."

He gave her a thoughtful look and held the door while she slid into the passenger seat in the front.

Jake slid behind the wheel of the car and turned to Silas. "Ready for our adventure?"

"Yes!" Silas held up his iPad. "And I can play games on this."

"You might want to watch for alligators as we cross Alligator Alley. I thought Noelle might like to see the Everglades." He turned to her. "Have you visited them?"

"Not really. We've flown over them but that's all."

"We?"

"A thing of the past," Noelle said and stared out the window at the passing scenery.

Jake remained quiet, while Noelle thought of all the exciting things she'd done with Alex. He'd loved to travel and had opened up a world to her of different places and excellent food. She'd thought it would always be that way—discovering new things together.

Her family had always lived a nice, middle-class life. Her parents loved her and her siblings and worked hard to provide for them. When the four kids were small, vacations were taken sparingly. Some summers, her parents rented a cottage on Cape Cod for two weeks, where meals and snacks could be eaten at home. Her mother was more than an adequate cook who tried to come up with tasty dishes for her growing family.

Noelle's memories ended abruptly when Jake pulled into a rest area. "Sorry. I have to take this call and didn't want to listen to it in the car." He climbed out of the driver's seat and stood nearby.

From where she was sitting, Noelle watched as Jake swiped his finger across the screen of his cell. The relaxed manner of a moment ago was lost as he talked on the phone. His back was straight, he waved his hand emphatically, and looked like what he was—an owner of a small, highly successful hotel chain. Three major hotels would give anyone cause to be uptight from time to time.

When Jake returned to the car, a scowl marred his brow. He slid behind the wheel and muttered, "Damn lawyers. Can't live with them or without them."

"A nuisance and a necessity," Noelle agreed. "One step at a time, I tell myself."

Jake let out a sigh. "You're right. With all that's gone on with my parents' disappearance, things have gotten crazy."

"I can well imagine," said Noelle. "I'd be heartbroken if anything like that ever happened to mine."

Jake was quiet a moment. Then after checking to see that Silas was wearing a small headset while watching a movie on his iPad, he said, "I keep telling myself it never happened, that they're still here, but then it all comes back. No one holds any hope of finding them alive."

"I'm sorry. I really am," said Noelle, moved by his confession.

"The one good thing about it is they were together. They were very close and would be unhappy without the other."

"That's so sweet," Noelle said.

"Yes. How rare is that?" The disgust in his voice caught her attention. *Someone must have hurt him. Claire?* She wasn't about to ask.

As soon as Jake pulled up to the porte cochère in front of the large, white-stucco hotel, a doorman hurried to greet them. While he spoke to Jake, another uniformed man opened the passenger door for her. "Welcome to the Bellingham Miami Beach. We hope you have a pleasant stay."

"Thank you," Noelle replied, gazing at the expanse of glass on either side of the entrance. Potted palms, and huge brown pots filled with bright-red and hot-pink geraniums softened the front walk and added a colorful welcome.

Silas stood with her while they waited for Jake to join them. Several pairs of eyes studied her, but she ignored them. She knew her place.

Inside, the lobby was brightly lit by crystal chandeliers shimmering in the sunlight streaming through the wall of glass that overlooked an outside lounge area and large swimming pool beyond. The sea-blue rug covering most of the lobby floor was accented with swirls of orange, red, and yellow. It was interesting but not overdone. In fact, Noelle thought as she looked around, everything about the hotel was tasteful—from the furnishings to the lighting and to the carved-wooden front desk overseeing it. A large, saltwater fish tank sitting along one of the walls was an added attraction. Colorful fish darted about in the turquoise water, luring both kids and adults to it.

Jake came up behind her. "We're all taken care of. Hope you don't mind, but we're not staying in the Presidential Suite. At two thousand dollars a night, we need to sell it rather than put us there."

"Believe me, that's no problem." Noelle and Silas followed Jake into a glass-sided elevator and stood together looking out as the elevator rose to the fourteenth floor, giving them a nice look at the property that sat on the sandy shores of the Atlantic Ocean.

"We're here," Jake said softly.

Noelle turned away from the glass and smiled. "It's beautiful, Jake."

His lips curved. "Glad you think so. It's my favorite property."

He wrapped an arm around Silas and motioned for her to come with them. They walked down a thick-carpeted hallway whose walls were papered in a subtle gold pattern. The darker gold of the carpet set off the walls nicely and would, Noelle supposed, hide a lot of wear from traffic.

Jake opened the door to the Heron Suite and motioned for her to go inside. Noelle stepped through the doorway and stopped in admiration. A sea of turquoise carpet met her feet. The palest of gold, almost-white color of the walls led the way to sliding-glass doors that opened onto a balcony overlooking the ocean. In the living area, two overstuffed couches and the chairs flanking them were covered with textured fabrics in white, turquoise, and soft gold. Orange pillows brightened the couches. Photos of decorative shells hung on the wall, and in the center of the glass coffee table between the two couches was a huge glass bowl full of shells of all kinds.

"This is lovely," said Noelle, earning a smile from Jake.

She saw that bedrooms opened up on either side of the living room and turned to look at the interior wall of the suite. A small breakfast table with two chairs sat beside a gray-marble counter that held a microwave, a small sink, and an under-counter dishwasher. A white refrigerator stood at one end matching the white-painted cupboards above the counter on either side of the sink.

"Look, Noelle! Seashells!" cried Silas, holding up a shell in front of her.

"Nice. We can study them right here," she said, placing a finger of warning to her lips.

Silas nodded his understanding and turned to his father. "Dad, can Noelle and I go to the pool now?"

Jake checked his watch. "I don't see why not. I have some business to take care of and dinner won't be for some time." He glanced at Noelle. "Sound okay to you?"

"Fine. It'll give me a chance to get a little sun before it sets. This late in the day is the best time for me to be outside without burning my skin."

His gaze swept over her. "Nice."

She blinked rapidly, wondering what that remark or his smile meant.

"I'll leave you two now and catch up with you later. Take whichever bedroom you want, Noelle, though I believe the suitcases have already been brought up and settled in our rooms."

After Jake left, Noelle said to Silas. "Remember, don't say anything to your father about seashells. Decorating your tree is our secret. I brought my book, and we can study some of the shells here in the suite. That'll make it easier."

Silas' eyes sparkled. "Another secret. I really like you, Noelle."

Noelle and Silas picked several shells out of the bowl on the coffee table and carried them into the bedroom where Noelle's suitcase had been placed. She got out her book on shells and identified a few shells—Scotch bonnets, olives, limpets, and a scallop.

"Do you think Dad will let me take them home?" asked Silas.

"You'll have to ask him," said Noelle. Even though Jake owned the hotel there was no way she'd encourage Silas to take something without permission.

"Can we go swimming now?"

"It's fine with me. The temperature has heated up just like the weatherman announced. I'll help you find your bathing suit and meet you in the living room."

For this trip, well aware that Jake would be too busy to sit by the pool with them, she'd brought her bikini.

Lying on a chaise lounge beside the pool, Noelle kept an eye on Silas. He seemed comfortable in the water doing somersaults and swimming across the pool in front of her. Swimming was something she encouraged all the residents of New Life to enjoy. She'd initiated a special exercise class for them and found those who participated on a regular basis were less likely to have physical ailments.

Silas came out of the water and sat beside her. "I'm through swimming. Can I play a game on my iPad?"

"Sure. It's right here in the beach bag we brought down from the room." She handed it to him.

With the soft sounds of Silas's online game in her ear, she

closed her eyes, reveling in that time between sleep and wakefulness, letting her thoughts drift in a sea of contentment.

"Still here?" came a deep voice above her.

Noelle jerked fully awake and sat up. Jake was standing by her chair, giving her a look that could be described only as sexy.

Fighting the childish urge to cover herself, Noelle got to her feet, grabbed the terrycloth robe the hotel had provided in the room, and wrapped it around her. "Guess it's time to get ready for dinner, huh?"

Jake checked his watch. "We've got a little time. Should we go up to the room and have a before-dinner glass of wine? I'm off duty, so to speak, so it's not inappropriate."

"That sounds lovely," said Noelle, pleased she was being treated as not just a nanny.

Still playing his computer game, Silas was easily led to the elevator and up to the room.

"Maybe I'd better change," said Noelle, wrapping the robe tighter around her.

"It's not necessary. I have one more thing to do before dinner but have a moment right now to relax. Have a seat out on the balcony. I'll open the bottle of wine I ordered and bring a glass of it to you."

"Okay." Her hair was windblown, and her skin was covered with suntan lotion, but if Jake didn't mind her appearance, she wasn't about to fuss. She wasn't out to impress him or anyone else here in Florida. She was on vacation to forget all about that kind of thing.

Jake came out to the balcony, handed her a glass of red wine, and sat in a chair opposite her. "I gave Silas juice and a snack. While he's all set with that and his game, I thought it would be a good time for me to get to know you a little better.

It's only been a few days, but you already seem part of the household."

She took a sip of her wine, letting its smoothness stroke her throat as she swallowed and gathered her thoughts. "I never expected to be in this situation. You could say it all started the day I met and fell in love with your son."

"You don't have kids of your own?" Jake asked.

"No, I've always wanted a big family, but things haven't worked out that way. I guess I just haven't found the right guy."

His gaze was steady as he leaned toward her and spoke softly. "What is all this business about money and not being paid? I have to admit it's a very unique experience for me."

Noelle hesitated, wondering how much to say.

"It comes from something unpleasant?"

Prompted, she nodded. "Let's just say I hate the way people with money think they can buy someone's affection or toss them away."

Jake leaned back in his chair. "I'll admit I was talking to a friend in Boston regarding your nursing background and he told me something about an engagement gone wrong."

Noelle's cheeks flamed with embarrassment. She fought the tears that stung her eyes. "There you have it. Me, a loser."

The look of sympathy that flashed across his face surprised her. "I can understand what you went through," Jake said. "Love gone wrong is painful. Now that I'm single again, you can imagine how many people are interested in me because of the hotels, not who I really am."

Noelle studied him. She hadn't thought of how the very things she didn't like about him might be the same things that hurt him.

"Tell me about your work," Jake said. "Your references were glowing. I'm very thankful you discovered what was happening to Nana. I'm sorry I didn't know."

Once Noelle began talking about her job and some of the people she worked with, conversation between them was easy. She was an excellent nurse with creative ideas, and she knew it. Noelle even told him about Edith Greenbaum and her cronies.

"You really are a natural nurturer." Jake's smile brightened his face and lit his eyes. "You remind me of a nanny Brett and I had growing up. Her name was Mrs. Jenkins. I loved her. After she stopped working for my family, I kept in touch. She died a few years ago. I still miss the way she could make me see things in a different way." Jake suddenly stopped talking. "My God! I haven't ever told anyone else that."

"That kind of relationship is very nice," said Noelle. "I had that with my grandmother."

"When Nana was better, she used to love to do things with Brett and me. It's sad to see how her memory is going." Jake's cell phone buzzed. He checked his watch and jumped to his feet. "Sorry. I've got an appointment. I'll be back in an hour to accompany you and Silas to dinner."

He rose and carried their empty glasses into the kitchen. Noelle followed him inside, checked on Silas, and then went to her bedroom to get ready.

Later, soaking in the luxurious deep tub, Noelle's thoughts remained on Jake. She didn't know what to think of him. Sure, he was a handsome, rich guy who'd carried his share of their conversation, but she knew there was a whole lot more to him.

As she soaped her skin, she vowed not to allow herself to get emotionally involved with either Jake or his brother. It wasn't a life she wanted. Her thoughts flew to the older dentist her mother had introduced her to and decided she didn't want that either.

Toweled off from her bath and dressed, Noelle stood in

front of the full-length mirror and studied the figure before her. The tiny blonde whose blue eyes stared back at her so critically had always been popular in school and later among the dating set. But she couldn't compare to the statuesque, skinny women who worked so hard to keep their shape. Hers was a natural beauty that was as open as her heart. Or so her mother had told her time and time again.

Noelle saw herself as she was—an attractive, young woman with no games to play. A light dusting of eye shadow and mascara enhanced her eyes, a soft coral lipstick colored her lips. She wore no other makeup. Not for a dinner with a man who thought of her as the nanny.

Still, she was glad the black dress she'd brought with her fit her curves nicely and the V-neckline was low enough to be of interest but tasteful. The diamond earrings she wore were shown to nice effect among the wispy curls of her hair.

When she entered the living room, she found Silas sitting beside the coffee table studying the shells. It touched her that he was so excited about the Christmas tree they were going to decorate together.

"I found another scallop shell. See?" He held up a pretty shell with pink markings.

Noelle smiled. "That's a good one."

A sound at the door to their suite caught her attention. She went to see who it was.

Jake's eyes widened when he saw her. "You look great."

Ignoring the look of surprise on his face, she smiled. "Thanks."

"Thought we'd eat right here at the hotel. It makes things easier," said Jake. "Besides, I'm hoping you'll help me try out some new items on the menu."

"You might be sorry. I'm a real foodie. I even like caviar and escargots."

His face once more registered surprise, but he nodded gamely. "How about I let you choose anything you want?"

"Deal," she said, holding out her hand. She might not want to be paid a lot of money, but it didn't mean she couldn't enjoy a few benefits that went with the job.

He laughed and shook her hand.

CHAPTER EIGHT

Her hand still tingling from the energy of the handshake she'd shared with Jake, Noelle was helped into her chair at a corner table in Jasper's, the upscale, American-cuisine restaurant at the hotel. She told herself the tingling meant nothing, but the rest of her body didn't quite believe her. Forcing herself to think of other things, she looked around the restaurant.

Through a section of glass wall, Noelle gazed out at the unobtrusive lighting that showcased the bright pink hibiscus blossoms in the bushes lining the wall's exterior and nearby palm trees. The fronds of the palms rustled and swayed in an onshore breeze. The dark waves of the water rolling in were tipped in white, like a lacy collar.

Observing the tropical scene, a sigh of pleasure escaped her lips.

"Pretty, huh?" said Jake.

"Lovely," she agreed. She loved Boston and the shoreline there, but the warmth and brightness of color in this setting was especially pleasing when she knew what weather awaited her when she returned home.

"All right. I said you can order anything you want, but if you're so inclined, would you think about ordering the sea bass or maybe the chicken? The chef is trying out a couple of new recipes, and I want to see how others like them. They've received both raves and disappointing comments. But it's important that he's changed things up a bit."

"Why don't I do the sea bass?" Noelle said.

Jake rewarded her with a smile. "Shall I order champagne? You said you liked caviar, and champagne would go well with it."

"No, thank you. Something simpler is fine for me right now."

"Okay, leave it to me. I've got a nice white wine in mind for us. I'll try the new chicken dish, and what I have in mind will be good with both." He turned to Silas. "What would you like, son? You usually get a burger, but do you want to try something new? The pasta might be something you'd like. We can ask for it with the seafood sauce or a plain red sauce."

"Plain red sauce, Dad," said Silas, "and, please, can I have chocolate cake for dessert?"

"Yes. You're just like your old man when it comes to chocolate cake," Jake said, beaming at him. He turned to Noelle. "The way they make it here is my favorite."

After their orders were placed and the wine steward had taken care of serving a nice sauvignon blanc, Jake sat back in his chair and raised his glass. "Here's to you, for being such a helpful neighbor."

Lifting her glass, she smiled. "And to having such nice neighbors."

As the sip of delicious, cool wine was sliding down her throat, a woman appeared at the table. Noelle noticed the panic in Jake's eyes and studied her.

Hair dyed much too bright above her wrinkled face, she appeared to be in her sixties.

"Long time no see, Jake. It's great to find you out and about again. I was so sorry to hear about your parents. Such a shame." She turned to Noelle and gave her a long, steady stare. "Mmm."

"Liz, it's nothing ..." Jake said, giving Noelle an apologetic look. "Noelle, this is Liz Connors. She writes a society column for one of the local social magazines."

"And who are you, dear?" said Liz, sounding like the spider talking to the fly in a familiar poem.

Recoiling, Noelle looked to Jake.

"She's the new nanny, Noelle North." Jake sent Noelle a second look of apology.

Though Noelle understood he was simply trying to make it clear that they had no social connection, his words stung.

"She's my friend," said Silas, staring at the woman with round eyes.

"And this is your son, Silas. My, he's growing fast." Liz smiled. "I won't keep you and Noelle from your toasting each other, Jake. Have a lovely evening together."

Noelle's stomach curled. Alex had always loved catching the attention of people like Liz, basking in the limelight of notoriety. Noelle was uncomfortable with it, as she was now.

"I'm sorry. I didn't want Liz to jump to any wrong conclusions," Jake said, after Liz left the table. "I pretty much try to stay out of the social circle stuff. Claire loved it, but I don't."

"Mom liked to wear crowns," said Silas.

Noelle glanced at Jake with surprise.

He grimaced. "Claire had a small tiara she wore to a couple of her big society events both here and in New York."

"I see," said Noelle quietly, wondering what kind of life Silas had led when both his parents were so busy—one with business and the other with all the trappings of high society.

She was relieved when their appetizers arrived.

"How do they look?" Jake asked, leaning over to study her Oysters Rockefeller.

"Perfect." Having grown up with simple food, a whole new world had opened up to her when she'd met Alex, a man who'd introduced her to the finest things, including fabulous food.

Oysters Rockefeller with their hollandaise sauce and other ingredients had become one of her favorite appetizers.

Well aware Jake was watching her, Noelle raised her seafood fork and lifted an oyster to her mouth. When she swallowed and then gave him a thumbs-up sign, he beamed at her.

"I'm glad you like Dad's food," said Silas. He had a tiny bit of red sauce at the corner of his mouth.

She reached over and dabbed at his lips with her black napkin. "Good food is one of life's pleasures," she said, quoting her father, who often proclaimed it after one of her mother's meals.

Noelle started to eat another oyster when she noticed Jake staring at her. "What?"

Looking uncomfortable, he shrugged. "It's a pleasure to watch you eat."

"Mom didn't like to eat. Right, Dad?"

Looking even more uncomfortable, Jake shifted in his chair and turned to Silas. "Your mother liked to eat, but she was very worried about gaining weight. Some people are like that."

Silas beamed at her. "But not Noelle."

Noelle couldn't hold back the chuckle that bubbled inside her. "I don't know whether to be embarrassed or not."

Jake laughed with her. "Let's all three of us enjoy the meal," he said with a twinkle in his eye, evaporating the earlier tension at the table.

During the meal, Jake answered her questions about the hotels he and his brother now oversaw and seemed pleased by her genuine interest. Noelle understood better the pressure he was under as he and Brett assumed the duties and responsibilities of running the hotels. Until his parents and their plane were found, the actual transfer of ownership had been put on hold.

Though Jake spoke with pride about the work he was doing, a sadness lingered on his face. Her heart went out to him. She couldn't imagine the difficult position into which he'd been placed. Miracles sometimes happen. Maybe his parents were alive somewhere. But even as she thought it, the basic facts made it seem impossible.

By the time coffee and dessert were served and eaten, Noelle was feeling relaxed and pleasantly sated with delicious food.

"I think we'd better get this little boy to bed," Jake said. "Ready to go?"

"Yes, it was delicious. Thank you very much."

He rose and went to her chair, beating out the waiter who'd been watching them. "My pleasure."

As they made their way out of the dining room, Noelle noticed people watching them and stayed close to Silas.

Upstairs, in their suite, she helped put Silas to bed and then headed to her own bedroom.

Jake approached her. "Thanks for everything, Noelle. It was a pleasant evening. I'll see you in the morning."

She entered her room and closed the door. Jake Bellingham had turned out to be a real gentleman. But she knew better than to try to make it more than it was. Besides, she'd seen what life was like on his social level, and she wanted nothing to do with it.

The next morning, while Jake was busy with work, she and Silas hung out at the pool, walked the beach in search of shells, and shared lunch at the poolside restaurant. Noelle realized how lonely a life it could be married to someone as engrossed in his work as Jake. Alex hadn't been as heavily involved in the financial advisory company his father owned.

The ride back to the Gulf Coast and Althea's house was quiet. Silas, his nose and cheeks pink from the sun, had fallen asleep in the backseat of the car. Jake spent most of his time on the car phone. Noelle tuned out his conversations by reading a book on her iPad.

Jake dropped her off at Seashell Cottage and thanked her once more for her help.

Inside the cottage, Noelle unpacked her suitcase and pulled on a pair of jeans and a sweatshirt from her college days. *This is more like it,* she thought, wiggling her toes on the rug inside her bedroom.

That night, as Noelle was pouring herself a glass of wine, she heard a knock on the door. Surprised, she went to answer it. Opening it cautiously, she peered out.

Jake stood in front of her. "May I talk to you for a minute?"

"Sure, Come in. I've just poured myself a glass of wine. Would you like one? It's a nice pinot noir."

Jake checked his watch. "Guess I'd better not. I just wanted to stop by to tell you that I've been called to New York for a couple of days. Silas tells me you're going to go to Nana's each morning to see him."

"Yes, I've agreed to do that for him to allow Dora time to help Althea prepare for the day."

He shuffled his feet like a nervous school boy. "There's something you'd better know. Liz Connors is making it appear on her society blog that you're more than my nanny. It's awkward, I know, considering your feelings toward me. I'm sorry it happened."

"Really? She did that?" Noelle's stomach filled with acid. "I hate that kind of publicity!" Noelle remembered how hurt she'd been in the past by such gossip and felt even sicker.

"Until things calm down, perhaps it's best if Silas comes

here for your get-togethers. This cottage isn't far away, and if Dora calls to let you know he's on his way, you could meet him."

"Okay, that sounds like a good way to prevent further speculation about us," Noelle said, wishing she'd never met him.

"Can you give me your phone number? I'll give it to Dora as well." Jake noticed her hesitation. "It won't be given to anyone else. I promise."

Noelle left him at the doorway to go into the kitchen for her cell. She returned, and they exchanged phone numbers.

"Thanks. One other thing. We can't let Silas think his friendship with you is anything more than a holiday treat. You keep saying how much you love your job and your family in Boston, and I wouldn't want him to get hurt by thinking you'd stay."

"Yes," Noelle replied crisply. "It's probably best to think that way."

His gray eyes studied her a moment. "You really are a nice person, Noelle. I hope you know how rare it is to find that in my world."

"I can imagine," she said softly. "Have a safe trip to New York."

"Thanks. I'd better go now."

She showed him out of the house and watched as he jogged down the sand as lithe and as handsome as his brother.

When she went back to the kitchen, she sank into a wooden chair at the table and let out a troubled sigh. Her carefully planned vacation of doing nothing had become very complicated. The last thing she wanted was for people to think she was Jake Bellingham's woman.

CHAPTER NINE

A couple of days later, Noelle followed her new routine and stood outside the cottage waiting for Silas to appear. If it weren't for him, Noelle would stop having any dealings with the Bellingham family. So far, she'd been told she was bossy, called a nanny, and asked not to get too close to Silas.

Yet, seeing that little boy run toward her with excited, leaping steps, she brushed away her irritation.

"Hi, Noelle! I brought a net bag with me for the shells," Silas said, racing up to her.

"Oh, good idea! I've got one too." They smiled at one another. "Let's head north, away from your house."

"Dora said to tell you there's a man at Nana's house. He's got a camera and wants to take a picture of you," said Silas. "Dora told him to go away, but he's still there. That's why she kept Duke at home."

Uneasiness streaked through Noelle's body. She did NOT want any kind of publicity. The press had devastated her once. That was more than was fair. She forced a smile and kept her voice light. "We'll find plenty of shells here."

Silas chattered with excitement as they strolled the beach, leaning over for a better view of the shells that lay at their feet. Watching Silas, Noelle couldn't help smiling to herself. On Sanibel Island, south of where they were, shell-seekers were described as doing the "Sanibel Stoop". Both Silas and she were "stoopers" now too.

After a while, they returned to Seashell Cottage. Noelle made Silas a peanut butter sandwich, and they sorted through the shells, choosing the ones they'd make into ornaments.

"Can we get the ribbons and the glue now?" asked Silas. "Dad said I could go with you."

Noelle called Dora. "Okay if I take Silas shopping? We're going to make a quick trip to one of the hobby stores. I'll return him home in an hour."

"That's fine with me. When you come here, the coast should be clear. Some guy from one of the local magazines was here to get a photograph of you. I told him you didn't live here."

"Thanks." Noelle hung up feeling better about her need for privacy.

When Noelle drove her car into the driveway at Althea's house, she was puzzled by the powder-blue convertible sitting alongside Dora's gray compact. She turned to Silas.

"Do you know whose car that is?"

He shook his head.

They walked inside the house and through the kitchen. Noelle could hear voices coming from the living room, and curious, followed the sound.

As Noelle stepped into the living room, a tall brunette jumped to her feet. Wearing tight white jeans, black high heels and a low-cut, black-knit top, she glared at Noelle. "You're Noelle North? Jake told me you weren't staying here."

Noelle stood her ground. "Who are you and why would you even care?"

"I'm Alicia Witherspoon," the woman said, her manner haughty. "And I care because I thought Jake and I had something special going on between us. He told me you weren't living here and that you had no interest in him. But seeing you now, I'm wondering if that's the truth."

"Well, as hard as it might be for you to believe either of us, it *is* the truth."

Silas took hold of Noelle's hand. "Noelle is my friend. We're making Christmas come to Nana's house."

Alicia turned her gaze onto him. "Is your Dad telling me the truth?"

"Don't answer," Noelle said, furious that Alicia would put Silas into such a difficult position.

"Well, is he?" said Alicia.

Silas shook his head. "No, he likes Noelle a lot. And I do too."

Alicia placed her hands on her hips and let out an angry breath. "That does it. I'll have to fly to New York and talk to him myself." She turned to Noelle. "You stay out of my business. Understand?"

A temper that rarely exploded inside Noelle burst out in strong, angry words. "I have no intention of being in your life or Jake's. Understand? I'm here for Silas and Althea. Now, if you'll excuse me, I have to leave." She gave Silas a quick hug and spoke to Dora. "Talk to you soon."

Quickly, before she could change her mind and expand on her frustration in dealing with Silas's father, she left the house, got in her car, and drove away. She checked her rearview mirror several times but saw no sign of a blue convertible behind her. At Seashell Cottage, Noelle parked her car and got out, breathing in the tangy, salty air and letting it out in a calming rhythm. What was it about Jake and his family that made life so difficult? Telling herself that it was only a matter of weeks until she was safely back in Boston, she unloaded her packages and carried them inside.

Later, she unrolled some of the red-and-green woven string Silas had selected for the ornaments. Practicing, she formed a loop and glued a portion of it to the back of a shell.

It was, she decided, a cute way to decorate a tree. Something new and different for her. Satisfied, she set the string and glue aside. Silas would help her with the rest.

She picked up a book, a new one by one of her favorite authors, and sat on the couch, happy for time to unwind. If Alicia Witherspoon was the type of woman Jake was interested in, that was another reason to keep out of his way until her promise to Silas was over.

She was deep into the book when her cell rang. Checking Caller ID, her spirits lifted.

"Hello, Edith! How are you and the gang doing?"

"Not as well as you, my dear. Looks like you might've snagged a really good one."

Noelle's heart pounded with dismay. "What do you mean?"

"You and Mr. Jake Bellingham. I was talking to a friend of mine in Miami. She loves those gossipy social blogs everyone reads, and when she saw a picture of you, she called me. Through my letters and photographs she knows who you are and what you look like."

Noelle's breath left her in a gasp. "You mean it's being circulated like that?"

"Hazel, Rose, and Dorothy are standing right here with me. I've got you on speaker phone. Now, tell us about it. How did you two meet? Do you think it's going to be one of those quick engagements, the meant-to-be kind of thing?"

"Whoa!" Noelle hated to be the one to shatter that kind of romantic thinking, but she had no choice. "Oh, my sweet ladies, it's nothing like that at all. I'm helping a little boy named Silas decorate a tree for Christmas. Silas is Jake's son, and I befriended his grandmother. That's it. Jake and I are definitely not suited for one another. He works all the time, has terrible taste in women, and belongs to a world I want no part of."

"Mmm. Doesn't sound very promising," said Dorothy.

"We might have to go for Plan B," whispered one of the women in the background.

"Thank you for your concern, ladies, but I came here to relax and get away from the holidays in Boston. I'm not looking for romance; I'm looking for peace and quiet, which has been elusive so far."

"Definitely Plan B," came another voice.

"I'm fine just the way I am," said Noelle, knowing full well it wasn't what the women wanted to hear. Who could blame them? They loved the idea of a romance. Three of them had been widowed for several years, and even though Hazel had never married, she was a devoted reader of romance novels.

"Well, we're here if you ever want to talk things over," said Rose.

Noelle's heart swelled with affection. "Thanks. I love you all."

After the goodbyes had been spoken, Noelle clicked off the call with a touch of homesickness. The four older women were dear to her.

Checking the clock in the kitchen, she saw that it was time to start fixing dinner. She liked fancy food, but something as simple as spaghetti was appealing too. She poured her evening glass of wine and took out the mushrooms she'd placed in the refrigerator, along with an onion and a red pepper. Adding those ingredients plus crushed fresh garlic to the contents of a jar of special sauce she'd bought at the gourmet store nearby would make a perfect, easy meal.

She set the prepared sauce to cook on low on the stove and took her wine out to the porch. Pulling her thick fisherman's sweater tighter around her, she plunked her sneakered feet up on the railing and sat back in a rocking chair, content to let time drift by. This was the kind of peace for which she'd been searching—a way to decide if she wanted to purchase the condo she'd been renting or go on a trip to Europe with her mother. Either would be a step forward. From inside, she could hear her cell phone ring and decided to ignore it. If it was an emergency, whoever it was would call her back.

Sighing with pleasure, she gazed at the stars in the sky, thinking of their timeless beauty and the miracle of them. She noticed the familiar belt of Orion and smiled, remembering camping outside in the backyard with her brothers. She'd had a nice childhood.

She jumped when a tall figure entered the field of light cast by the lamps inside the cottage. Her heart pounding, she stared at the figure approaching her, readying herself for a quick retreat.

"Noelle? I tried calling you, but you didn't answer. I took a chance and decided to walk here. I need the exercise anyway."

She clutched her hands to her chest. "Jake? You scared me! I thought you were the guy wanting to take my photo."

"What?"

"You know, the guy that works for the social magazine. Liz probably sent him. I'm not happy about it."

Jake climbed the stairs to the porch. "I'm sorry. That's why I'm here. I want to apologize to you."

She let out a sigh. "It's not your fault. I've poured myself a glass of wine. Would you like one?"

"Sounds great. Silas has already had dinner, and I wasn't ready to eat quite yet."

They went into the kitchen together. While Noelle poured the wine, Jake said, "Mind if I look around?"

"Not at all. I love this cottage. It's perfect for a beach getaway."

Jake was standing in the living room when Noelle found him.

"What do you think?" she asked as she handed him a glass of wine.

"I love it. Two buddies and I rented a beach house in college similar to this. Those were the best days of my life—all that fun and none of today's worries."

"Have a seat," said Noelle. "I just put frozen appetizers in the oven to bake. Thought we could share those. And if you'd like to stay for dinner, I've put together a spaghetti sauce and I can make a salad."

"Sounds great." The smile that spread across Jake's face gave Noelle pleasure. She could sense how troubled he was about everything happening in his life.

"Do you like to cook?" Jake asked.

"Brett knows I'm not very good at it. But since being here, I've decided I'm going to learn to do more than the basics. Maybe it's finally having some time to myself, but it seems like an excellent idea. Especially if I'm going to be alone."

"What's this about being alone?"

"Oh, it's nothing but my deciding I'm not going to get into any relationship any time soon. I hate the dating scene."

Jake cleared his throat. "Speaking of that, I understand you've met Alicia Witherspoon."

Noelle rolled her eyes. "She's convinced there's something going on between us and told me to stay out of her business. I tried to explain, but she didn't believe me."

"She and Claire could be twins in both looks and attitude," Jake said. "I've been upfront with Alicia about any future together, but she's not listening."

"I take it that you and Claire—"

"—were not getting along when she died. She wanted a divorce," Jake said bluntly, lowering his head. When he lifted his eyes to hers, a sadness lingered there. "Silas doesn't know she was about to leave both of us behind. I don't want to do or say anything to destroy his love for his mother."

"That's very generous of you," Noelle said. "I know how much you love your son."

A brightness came to his face. "Yes, he's the best thing in my life. This Christmas decorating idea of his is in memory of his mother. I thought you should know that."

"I won't do anything to take away from that," Noelle assured him before rising and going into the kitchen. Jake followed her.

Noelle put a pot of water on to boil for the spaghetti and pulled out lettuce from the refrigerator. She held up an old salad dressing bottle. "I'm not sure I've got enough."

"No problem. Want me to put together a salad dressing?" Jake asked. "All I need is olive oil, vinegar, garlic, dry mustard, a little salt and pepper, and a touch of curry."

She opened the cupboard. "Go ahead and check. The cottage was advertised as having a very complete kitchen."

He poked in the cupboard and turned to her with a triumphant grin. "We're all set. Hand me a salad bowl, and I'll whip up a dressing you won't believe."

Noelle poured more wine into their glasses and watched as Jake mixed the ingredients.

"Wow! You do know how to cook. Brett told me you're great at it."

Jake smiled. "It's a form of relaxation for me. When I'm home I like to do it."

"I'm impressed." Noelle lifted her glass and clicked it against Jake's. "Here's to good health and good food."

"Yes, for us both."

Noelle was surprised by how at ease Jake was with her. Perhaps it was knowing that they had no real interest in a future together that made it possible. Whatever the reason, she found herself enjoying his company.

After the meal ended, Jake checked his watch. "I'd better go. I promised I'd tuck Silas into bed. It's important to both of us for me to do that as often as I can."

"I understand. No problem making your way back home? Or I can drop you off at your house."

"Are you sure? That would be great."

Noelle grabbed her purse and car keys and led him out to the driveway where she'd parked her rental car.

An easy silence filled the car as she made the short trip to his house. When she pulled into the driveway of Althea's house, a powder-blue convertible was sitting there.

Jake let out a groan. "Guess I'm going to have to deal with her. Thanks for the ride. See you later."

"Good luck." Noelle waited until Jake was out of the car and then quickly drove away. She had no desire to deal with Alicia or have reason to question her own feelings regarding Jake.

CHAPTER TEN

Following her evening with Jake, Noelle made a firmer commitment to helping Silas with his Christmas project. The reason behind his enthusiasm was touching. He missed his mother and needed to remember happy times with her. For him, she'd play along. Each day when they grew tired of shelling or gluing, they did other things. Noelle had never had time for online games, but with Silas's encouragement soon found herself competing with him.

She remained aware of the need for Silas to understand she would be leaving in a few weeks, so she often talked about her family and the women at the assisted-living community. In return, he shared that he didn't like his school in New York. And when he talked about other kids being mean, she understood and decided to speak to Jake about it.

One day when Noelle and Silas were walking on the beach, a little girl who looked about Silas's age rushed over to them. "What are you doing?"

"Looking for seashells," said Silas importantly.

"Can I come too?" she asked.

Noelle smiled at her. "What's your name?"

"Grathie Thmith."

A woman strolled over to them. "Hello. I'm Sylvia Smith. Is Gracie bothering you?"

"Not at all," said Noelle. "I'm Noelle North and this is Silas Bellingham. I was about to ask if Gracie would like to come with us to look for shells. We won't be long and we won't go far."

Gracie tugged on her mother's hand. "Mom, pleathe let me go with them."

"How about I come too?" said her mother. "I need the exercise."

Noelle smiled at her. "That would be lovely. Then we can get to know one another." As Gracie and her mother moved forward looking for shells, Silas stayed in place, frowning.

"What's the matter?" Noelle asked.

"She's a girl and she talks funny," Silas said in a loud whisper.

"Gracie seems like a very nice little girl. You need to give her a chance to prove it," Noelle said sternly. "Come on. Let's go."

Noelle sent a look of apology to Gracie's mother as she and Silas approached.

"You can go ahead Gracie," said Sylvia. "But don't go too far."

"And I'll hold onto anything you find," Noelle offered, showing Gracie the big pocket in her coverup.

Silas hesitated for just a moment, then rushed forward. "Don't take all the good ones."

Noelle and Sylvia looked at one another and laughed.

"Kids. How many do you have?" Sylvia asked.

"None," Noelle replied, feeling a pang of disappointment. "I'm just helping out a family by spending time with Silas. Though, honestly, he's wormed his way into my heart."

"He's a darling little boy. I'm glad to see Gracie has found a friend. She's been having problems at school because of her lisp. We have her in speech therapy but it takes time to learn to speak differently."

"I don't understand where all the meanness is coming from," said Noelle. "I don't see it in the older people I'm working with, but some of their young visitors can be downright cruel. I don't get it."

"They've started a kindness program at Gracie's school, but it still hurts to be marked differently." Sylvia shook her head. "There's a little girl in Gracie's class who imitates her. It's very hurtful. But it's important that Gracie is able to stand up for herself. I can't be running into the school to defend my daughter all the time."

"Yes, I understand," said Noelle.

As the kids collected shells, Noelle and Sylvia were becoming acquainted. From outside New York City, Sylvia was a stay-at-home mom with Gracie and twin brothers who were just ten months old. She listened eagerly as Noelle told her about her job at the assisted-living community.

"Sounds interesting," said Sylvia. "I thought about being a nurse once, but then life and a guy named Rob happened."

At that moment, Silas came running to Noelle, holding his bag in the air. "I've got enough shells for today. Can we go home now?"

"Let's see what you have." Noelle peered into his bag. "Looks like you found some very nice ones."

"It's time for us to go back, anyway," said Sylvia. "We have a nanny, but it's not fair to leave her alone with the twins for too long."

Silas looked up at Gracie's mother and took Noelle's hand. "Noelle is my nanny."

At Sylvia's look of surprise, Noelle said, "It's complicated."

Sylvia laughed. "Yes, I'm sure. I'm so glad we met. See you later." She turned to Gracie. "Say goodbye to Silas."

Gracie waved. "'Bye, Thilath."

"'Bye," Silas said. He didn't look at her as he rubbed a bare foot back and forth in the sand.

After they'd walked away, Noelle said to Silas, "Let's sit a moment."

When they were both settled on the ground, Noelle turned to Silas. "I know you didn't want to be with Gracie, but I think you should remember to be kind. Playing with a girl shouldn't matter and neither should how she talks matter to you. She was polite and kind to you. Why couldn't you be kind to her?"

Silas shrugged.

"Remember the kids at your school who are sometimes mean to you?"

Silas made a face and nodded.

"How did that make you feel? Good?"

"Unh-unh."

"Remember that, Silas. Now, I'd better walk you home. It's getting late."

On the walk home, Silas was quiet. Noelle let him be, hoping he was thinking about Gracie.

She saw that Silas was safely inside the house and went to visit Althea. With more activity around her and the exercises her new physical therapist was doing with her, Althea seemed much more alert and happier.

Noelle was sitting and holding Althea's hand, chatting, when Jake came into the room.

"May I talk to you, Noelle?" he said in a commanding voice.

"Sure. I'll be right there," she replied.

"Now," Jake said.

Stiffening at the way he'd spoken to her, Noelle rose and faced him. "What is the problem?"

"I need to talk to you about something," he said, glancing at his grandmother.

Noelle leaned down and gave Althea a kiss on the cheek. "I'll see you later."

Outside, Althea's room, Noelle turned to Jake. "You were rude to me. I don't appreciate it."

Jake's mouth dropped. "You work for me. Remember?"

"I'm a friend to Silas and Althea. That's it." She glared at him. "And I do it for free. So, no, I don't work for you."

Jake held up both hands and backed away. "Sorry. Sorry. It's just that Silas is crying and I need to find out why. He says it's your fault."

"Yes, if teaching him to be kind is my fault, so be it. I talked to him about treating a little girl with a lisp kindly. That's it. I'm going now before I say something I may regret."

She moved past him, out of the house, and onto the beach, as angry as she'd ever been. Breaking into a run, her feet pounded the sand in a steady beat until she finally slowed.

"Jake Bellingham is the most frustrating man I've ever met," she declared to the sandpipers scurrying along the sand, sending them rushing to get away from the anger in her voice.

Noelle laughed at their antics, releasing the feelings that battled inside her. She couldn't deny she was attracted to Jake at the same time he annoyed the crap out of her. Boston seemed so safe, so boring.

Back at the cottage, Noelle looked up a recipe online for a chicken dish. As she'd told Jake, she was determined to become a better cook. And she'd found that once she was into making something new, she enjoyed it.

She decided on a lemon chicken recipe and made a list of things she'd need to buy. As she was driving to the store, she thought about her life choices and why she'd be careful in the future. She'd been young and foolish about so many things—boyfriends, wanting material things, being swayed by the opinion of others. Some women didn't like being in their thirties, but Noelle was finding it liberating.

Feeling better about her day, she parked the car and entered the Seaside Gourmet market with a spring in her step.

She'd just picked up a couple of lemons in the produce department when she heard a familiar voice behind her. "You going to add any sugar to those lemons?"

Noelle whipped around to find Brett grinning at her.

"What are you doing here in Florida? I thought you had to be in New York."

"I came home for a break. New York is exhausting. I need a couple days of sunshine and sea air. Right now, I'm picking up some of Nana's favorite treats for her."

"Understandable," Noelle said.

"What are you making?" Brett asked. "Anything interesting?"

She laughed and placed her hands on her hips. "Are you hinting for an invitation to dinner?"

"I thought of it," he admitted sheepishly.

"Come to Seashell Cottage at six thirty. I'm trying something new."

His look of surprise brought another soft laugh out of her. "I've decided to learn how to cook more adventuresome things."

"Guess you can teach an old dog new tricks, huh?"

She swatted him. "Are you sure you're not one of my brothers incognito?"

He laughed. "Just keeping you on your toes. I'll see you at six thirty."

She watched him leave, thinking it would be nice to have a pleasant evening with a man who had no interest in her beyond being a friend. Though she hadn't intended to do so, she realized she'd been stuck in an emotional limbo for the past two years, wondering if she'd ever find a decent man. Now she was thinking of other things—improving her cooking skills, perhaps following through on requests to speak to various groups and classes about elder abuse, and learning to enjoy simple things like reading novels, walking the beach, and discovering quiet moments. But her main focus at the moment was helping a little boy celebrate Christmas—the one thing she'd hoped to avoid.

She'd just finished putting the casserole together and was about to clean up the mess she'd made when her cell phone rang. She checked Caller ID. *Brett.*

"Don't tell me you're backing out of dinner," she teased. "I've just finished making it."

"Uh ... actually, that's why I'm calling. There's an emergency in New York, and I'm flying up there this evening. Can we make it for another time?"

"Sure, I understand," she said, unable to hide her disappointment.

"I've spoken to Jake and he said he'd love to take my place. He's been stuck in the office here all day. I'm sure he'd like to get away for a while."

She hesitated.

"Sorry. Didn't mean to put you on the spot like that. I'll tell him to forget it," said Brett. "I do hope, though, we can make it another time. I'm a very competent test taster of homecooked meals."

Noelle smiled. He sounded just like her brother Mike. And what harm would it be to have an evening with Jake? Maybe they could make it through dinner without getting on each other's nerves. "Brett? Tell Jake I'll see him at six thirty. Have a safe trip."

"Thanks."

Noelle clicked off the call, hoping her new recipe turned out well. Brett would be easily satisfied, but Jake was a good cook and would know right away if she messed up. She didn't like the idea of disappointing him or herself.

After cleaning up the kitchen, Noelle went into her

bedroom to change her clothes. With Brett, she might've stayed in her jeans. But Jake was always so properly dressed, she decided to put on a clean pair of slacks and a blue sweater that everyone had told her matched the blue in her eyes. Her mother always told her it never hurt to look nice.

CHAPTER ELEVEN

Noelle tried not to feel nervous as she went to answer the knock on the door. But cooking for other people was new to her. She told herself that, and not seeing Jake, was the reason for the flutter in her stomach. When she opened the door and saw Jake standing there in a crisp, plaid shirt and pressed, khaki pants, she was glad she'd taken a little extra time with herself. Her hair, normally a curly mess, was nicely brushed and her eyes enhanced with mascara and eye shadow.

"Thanks for having me for dinner," Jake said, and handed her a bottle of white wine. "Thought this might go with whatever lemony thing you're cooking."

Noelle smiled and accepted the bottle from him. "Come on in. Guess Brett filled you in on what I am attempting to do."

Jake chuckled quietly. "Cooking isn't as hard as some people think. If you're good at math, can figure out what works, and change it up a bit, you have a chance of making something tasty."

"It's the changing it up thing that worries me. My mother just seems to throw things in a bowl, mix it up, and bake it, and it comes out perfect."

"Ah, my mother was the same way when she was home long enough to prepare dinner."

Noelle heard the sadness in his voice and said, "It will be interesting to see how this comes out. If it's too awful to eat, we can always have cereal or scrambled eggs."

Jake pretended to shudder. "I'm sure it won't come to that."

Noelle remained quiet. There'd been plenty of evenings when cereal or an egg was exactly what she'd fixed for dinner.

"Would you like me to pour the wine?" Jake said.

"Yes, that would be nice. I've set out two glasses on the counter along with an opener."

Jake grinned. "You're well-prepared, I see."

"Be prepared is one of my mottos from way back when. And in my business, it's important to be ready for anything."

Jake's expression grew serious. "I'm sorry about snapping at you earlier. It's been a tough few weeks at work, and something's happening with Silas that I don't understand. He's talking more about his mother, arguing with me, and crying over stuff that never used to bother him."

"Hmmm. I'm sorry to hear that. Gracie is a little girl Silas and I met on the beach. When she asked to join us looking for shells, Silas told me he didn't want to be with her because she's a girl and talked funny. I spoke to him about being kind. He might have been ashamed but that's all. As I mentioned earlier, some of the kids at school have bullied him. It could have something to do with not having a mother. I don't know the details, but I think you should be aware of it. I wanted to tell you this earlier, but never had the chance."

Jake let out a long sigh. "I know he's missing his mother, but I'm not about to plunge into another serious relationship right away. I can't do that. Someone who might make a great mother for Silas might not make a suitable wife for me. I'm sure you understand."

"I do indeed," she answered.

They exchanged smiles.

"Now that we have an understanding of our futures, how about some wine?" Noelle said in an attempt to lighten up the conversation.

Jake poured the wine and raised his glass to hers. "Here's

to us! May we never rush into a relationship!"

Laughing, they clicked glasses.

"Let's sit in the living room," Noelle said after taking a sip of the wine. "I think we'll be more comfortable there."

"Sounds great. I've been studying numbers all day, and staring at a lovely woman will be a very nice change." He winked at her.

Knowing the compliment didn't mean anything, Noelle smiled. She'd have a very nice view too.

As she sat in a chair facing him on the couch, Noelle was curious about the man whose son she loved. "You talked about your mother cooking whenever she could. Is that how you learned? With her?"

Jake shook his head. "No, I hung around the kitchen of the New York hotel. One of the sous chefs worked with me from time to time, and then I took a couple of cooking classes thinking I might like to own a restaurant one day. But if you want to have success, owning a restaurant can be even more time consuming than owning a hotel. And, besides, I knew Brett and I would end up running a hotel one day. I just didn't think it would be like this—with my parents missing and overseeing three hotels, not one."

"And now, I suppose, you expect Silas to come into the business when he's older."

"I hope so." Jake shrugged. "But only if that's what he wants. At one time, I thought I'd have a large family and those of my children who wanted to be a part of the hotel world would be. But life got in the way."

"So, you have other people manage them for you?"

"Oh, yes. We've found capable people to manage the hotels, but we still must oversee the operations. So many things can go wrong or get off track. I'm finding that as my father aged, he didn't pay attention to some things that should have been turned over to Brett or me."

"You're the numbers guy and Brett more the PR guy?"

Jake smiled. "Yeah, I'm the boring brother."

Noelle's lips curved. She was well aware that most women would consider him anything but boring.

"Tell me about your family," said Jake, leaning forward with interest.

Noelle found it easy to talk about the people she loved and how she was considered the spoiled baby sister by her three rowdy, older brothers. By the time the oven buzzer rang, Jake was laughing at the stories of how the four of them had caused such havoc for the parents who loved them equally.

Warmed by the memories, Noelle left the living room to finish dinner preparation in the kitchen.

Jake followed her. "Anything I can do to help?"

Noelle looked around. "Pour water into the goblets, and if we want more wine, I've got a bottle in the refrigerator you can open."

"Water and wine. I can do that."

While he did so, Noelle cooked frozen peas, fluffed the rice she'd cooked earlier, and made sure all was ready to serve. Swallowing nervously, she pulled the dish out of the oven. Previously, she'd sautéed chicken breasts in a mixture of butter and olive oil, crisping their skin. A sauce of brown sugar, lemon juice, white wine, and a few other surprise ingredients like Angostura bitters was poured over the chicken breasts to keep them moist while slices of lemon placed on top added the piquant flavor she was looking for.

"Smells delicious." Jake came up behind her and placed a hand on her shoulder, leaning over to inhale the aroma.

She turned to thank him and almost met his mouth.

His eyes widened and he quickly stepped away.

Telling her heart to stop racing, she turned back to the

chicken dish. "I'll serve and keep any leftovers warm for seconds."

"Great," said Jake. "I'll help you."

As they worked to fill their plates, it was almost comical how carefully they avoided contact with one another. When they were finally seated opposite each other at the kitchen table, Noelle relaxed, calming the rebellious streak of heat that had shot through her at the idea of kissing him.

Noelle took a bite of her food and looked over at Jake. He was smiling. "Great chicken dish. Nice work, Noelle."

Satisfaction made her smile. She happily chewed and swallowed. It was delicious.

They ate in silence for a while, enjoying their food.

Then Jake gave her a worried look. "Do you think I should have Silas see a psychologist? Maybe talk about the ways he's missing his mother?"

"I can't speak as a parent, but I can tell you as a medical person that it is sometimes very helpful for a child to be able to talk to someone about his feelings. If you want, I'll try to get a better understanding of what is bothering him. But I'm not a professional."

"Any knowledge you can give me would be helpful. Then I can decide from there. I've never seen him take to anyone as quickly as he has to you. It's almost as if you two have a special connection. I'm not sure I understand it."

"It is unusual. Maybe he understands that I'm here only temporarily and, therefore, I'm not a threat to the status quo."

Jake nodded thoughtfully. "Maybe that's it. He certainly hasn't liked any of the women I've dated." He paused. "Not that I've done a whole lot of dating. Mostly, it's because I've needed someone to accompany me to some social function or another."

"Shelling is a good time to talk to Silas about lots of things.

If I discover any information you should have, I'll definitely let you know."

"Thanks. I appreciate it."

The chirping on Noelle's cell phone indicated a call. She glanced at Jake. "Excuse me. I'd better get this. If it's my mother and I don't answer, she'll ask too many questions."

He laughed, and she rose and went to her cell. When she saw the name on caller ID, her heart skipped a breathless beat. *Hazel Vogel.*

"Hello, Hazel! What's up?" Noelle held her breath. Hazel didn't like to use her cell phone and would call only in an emergency.

"It's Edith! She's had a heart attack. We don't know if she'll make it." Hazel's voice was wobbly with emotion.

"Oh my God! I'll get there as fast as I can. Keep your phone with you, Hazel. I'll call to let you know my plans." Noelle hung up and gripped the kitchen counter, dizzy with the blood draining from her face.

Jake jumped to his feet and hurried over to her. "What is it? Can I help?" His arms came around her, and she leaned into his chest and allowed her tears to flow.

"It's one of my people at the assisted-living community. Edith and I have a very sweet relationship. She's had a heart attack. A bad one. I need to get to her. I've got to catch a flight out of here as soon as possible."

"Have a seat and let me make a call," Jake said in a quiet, commanding voice.

Her mind racing, prayers on her lips, she collapsed into a kitchen chair. She couldn't lose Edith. Noelle had promised Edith she'd be with her at the end, but neither of them had expected that to happen anytime soon.

Noelle was still in a daze when Jake took a seat near her and clasped her hand. "It's all set. I've arranged for a private jet to fly you to Boston. I'll go along and be dropped off in New York. I needed to make a short trip there anyway."

Noelle straightened with surprise. "You'd do that for me?"

"Yes, of course. I understand how much it means to you to be there for your friend." He smiled at her. "If I can help you, I'm happy to do so."

Without stopping to think, she rose, threw her arms around him, and kissed his cheek. Then, realizing what she'd done, she pulled back. "Sorry. I forgot myself. What time is the flight?"

"As soon as we can make it happen. I don't need to pack. But I do need to go home and talk to Dora and say goodbye to Silas. Call me when you're ready, and I'll pick you up. We'll fly out of St. Pete-Clearwater International."

"Thank you. It shouldn't take me long to pack and lock up the cottage."

Noelle climbed the steps into the Cessna Citation jet that, apparently, was often used by the Bellingham family. Stepping inside, she felt like a VIP of great importance. Alex had been showy and extravagant, but he'd never chartered a private jet for her.

Inside, she sat down in one of the seven cushy leather chairs and picked up the bottle of water that had been placed nearby. She'd called Hazel and told her she was on her way and found out that Edith had been taken to the Newton-Wellesley Hospital.

"Comfortable?" Jake asked, sitting in a seat across the aisle from her.

She returned his smile. "This is the way to travel."

He laughed. "Flying like this saves a lot of time, and that's important. Sit back, relax and enjoy the trip. I'm going to review some paperwork."

As the jet flew through the sky, dark now, Noelle stared out the window and thought of Edith and the small group of ladies she'd organized. She loved them dearly. She'd found in dealing with the elderly that their view of the world was often contrary to modern-day ideas, and she was enlightened because of it. Many had experienced disappointment, heartbreak, and disease, but the inner strength they showed her was inspiring.

She thought of Edith. Right after Noelle had suffered the humiliating experience of being ditched at the church, Edith had spoken to her about moving on and had continued to reach out to her through the following news-media disaster. In return, Noelle listened as Edith talked about her rough life growing up, marrying an abusive man, and the peace she finally achieved. With both of Noelle's own grandmothers gone, Edith became the wise grandmother she needed.

Noelle leaned back in her seat and fell into a restless sleep. She awoke to hear the announcement that they were about to land at Hanscom Field north of Newton.

Jake reached over and tapped her arm. "Don't worry about transportation to the hospital. I've arranged for a limo to take you there. It's waiting for you now."

Filled with the fear that Edith might not make it, tears filled Noelle's eyes. "How can I ever thank you?"

"No need. Think of all you've done for Silas. I'd call it an even deal."

Noelle realized what was happening and said, "So you're paying me after all?"

He grinned. "Let's just say we're even now."

Her lips curved at the twinkle in his eye. "Okay, thanks."

After they deplaned and walked through the terminal, Noelle stepped into frigid air. At her side, Jake said, "There's the limo I ordered for you. Let me know how things go. Here's my phone number."

"You aren't staying?"

"No, like I said, I'll fly on to New York and spend a couple of days there."

She took the card he gave her and gave him a quick hug. "Thanks for everything. I'll let you know about Edith."

He stood by while the driver took Noelle's overnight bag and helped her into the limo. Then Jake hurried back into the terminal.

Her voice shaking, Noelle told the driver where she was headed.

"Yes, Ma'am. I know. Mr. Bellingham told me. He's already taken care of payment."

A guardian angel," Noelle thought, touched to the core by Jake's kindness.

As they pulled up to the front of the Newton-Wellesley Hospital, Noelle stared up at the brick front and whispered a silent prayer for Edith.

She stepped out onto the pavement, took hold of her suitcase, and entered the building.

At the reception desk, she explained who she was and asked about Edith Greenbaum.

"She's in Intensive Care for further observation."

"May I see her?"

"Are you a family member?"

"I'm listed as Edith's emergency contact."

The woman behind the desk said, "I'm sorry. I'll have to check with the nurses there."

Noelle tapped her foot nervously while the woman made a call. "It's fine for you to see her. Here." The woman handed her a sheet of paper with printed directions to the Intensive Care Unit.

Noelle quickly read them and then took off for the ICU on the third floor.

The nurse on duty behind the desk listened as Noelle introduced herself. "Hello. I got a call from reception. Yes, you're listed as her emergency contact, and it's noted that medical information can be released to you. She was admitted twenty-four hours ago and is resting right now. Before you see her, let me check to see if she's ready for a visitor."

"Can you tell me how she is? I'm a nurse so I want all the details."

"Oh. Okay. Her chart indicates a typical STEMI heart attack—ST-elevation myocardial infarction. Her ECG indicates damage but not as extensive as suspected. She was given clot-busting medication along with others and has undergone angioplasty and stenting. Overall, a pretty typical patient who is doing well." A smile brightened the nurse's face. "A feisty old gal."

Relief weakened Noelle's knees. She braced herself against the desk and drew a couple of deep breaths.

"Are you all right?" asked the nurse.

Noelle smiled and nodded. "Just feeling the effects of relief. I love that woman."

"I understand. She's a sweetie. Let me check on her, and I'll be right back."

As soon as the nurse gave her the signal, Noelle walked over to Edith's compartment and stepped inside. Asleep, Edith looked much older and smaller than Noelle remembered.

She went to her bedside. "Edith? It's me. Noelle." She bent down and kissed Edith's cheek.

Edith's eyes fluttered open. She reached up and touched Noelle's curls. "At first, I thought you were an angel coming to get me. You look like one, you know."

Noelle's eyes welled with tears. "I'm no angel, and you know it. But enough about me. How are you?"

"Doing okay. At least that's what the doctors tell me. I have no intention of leaving this life for a while yet."

"I'm glad. I was so afraid when Hazel called to tell me what happened. She said they didn't know if you'd make it."

Edith shook her head. "You know Hazel. She always sees the worst in any situation. I told her not to call you, that it was important for you to be away."

Noelle squeezed Edith's hand. "She knew I'd be furious if anything happened to you and she didn't tell me. As it was, I got here as soon as I could."

"How's your new young man?"

"If you're talking about Jake Bellingham, he's not my new young man even though he flew me up here on a private jet. He said he was going to go to New York and would drop me off here. Nice, huh?"

"A lovely gesture from someone who must really care about you."

"No, it's not like that at all," said Noelle. "I've been working on a holiday project with his son. The trip was sort of payback for the help I've given the family. Neither one of us is interested in a serious relationship."

Edith studied her. "Plan B it is then."

"What is this plan B I've heard you ladies talk about?" said Noelle, eying Edith suspiciously.

Edith smiled. "Nothing for you to worry about, sweet girl."

The nurse came to the compartment and spoke softly. "It's way past visiting hours. Time to go."

Noelle got to her feet. "Keep up the nice work, Edith. I and the other women are counting on you to keep us on our toes."

Edith's lips curved. "I should be home in a day or two, and then, look out!"

Noelle gave her another kiss. "I'm so very, very happy that you're doing this well. I'll see you tomorrow. I want to be here in the morning when the doctor makes his rounds. I'll let him know that I intend to make sure you're following all his rules for a long-term recovery."

"No more sneaking treats from the kitchen?"

Noelle shook a finger at her. "Nope. We're going to get you well and keep you that way for a long, long time."

Outside the hospital, Noelle waited for a cab to take her to her condo. The release of adrenaline from her body made her feel almost sick with fatigue. It was hard to believe that it hadn't been too many hours ago that she and Jake were enjoying dinner together.

CHAPTER TWELVE

The next morning, Noelle turned off her alarm and scrambled out of bed. She didn't want to miss meeting the doctor handling Edith's case. Edith had seemed remarkably well, but Noelle was aware how fast that could change. Once Edith was released and back home with proper oversight, Noelle felt she could return to Florida where a little boy was waiting for her.

Entering the hospital at eight o'clock as the night nurse had suggested, Noelle found her way to the ICU to meet the doctor handling Edith's case.

When she arrived on the third floor, an older gentleman stood at the nurse's station, making notes in a chart.

"Hello? Are you Dr. Goodwin?"

At his nod, Noelle added, "I'm Noelle North, here to see you about Edith Greenbaum."

"All right. Let's talk."

Dr. Goodwin briskly answered Noelle's questions and assured her that Edith was doing well and would be released late that afternoon, provided the assisted-living community where she lived would be able to attend to Edith's needs. Noelle explained her role there and told him she already had nursing staff lined up for just this kind of emergency.

After thanking Dr. Goodwin for talking to her, Noelle went to Edith's bedside feeling encouraged. She hugged Edith hello and told her the happy news that sometime late in the afternoon she'd be allowed to go home.

"I'll pick you up and take you to New Life," Noelle said,

automatically straightening the sheets and blanket on Edith's bed.

After chatting a while, Noelle stood. "I'm off to do a few errands. I'll see you later this afternoon." She bent to give Edith a quick kiss on the cheek.

Edith clasped her hand and looked up at her with a tender expression. "You've told me how your mother always calls you her Christmas angel, Noelle. You truly are, dear one."

"Ah, that's sweet, Edith. But you know I'd do anything for you."

Noelle's heart was still full from her conversation with Edith as she made her way out of the hospital to her car. She pulled the phone out of her purse and called her mother.

"Mom? I'm back in Boston for the day and would love to meet you for lunch. Any chance you're free?"

"For you, I'm always free. What's going on?"

"I'll tell you at lunch. Let's meet at the Square Café in Newton at noon. That will give me time to do a little shopping."

"See you then," her mother said.

Noelle called Jake's cell and left a message that Edith was doing better than expected and would return to the New Life Assisted-Living Community later that day. She assured him she would fly to Florida tomorrow to be there for Silas.

After shopping at the mall for personal items, Noelle stopped at her favorite bookstore to pick up some things for Silas. She imagined him alone, waiting for her return and wanted to take him some gifts. Among the collection of posters, crafts, and books, she found a treasure trove of art projects, books on the ocean, fish, and shells, along with a poster featuring a variety of shells. Excited to be able to surprise Silas, she left the store, went to her car, and called Dora.

"Hi, Noelle! I heard about your friend. I hope everything is all right," Dora said.

"Yes, she's going to be fine. But I need to talk to Silas. Is he there?"

"Right beside me. He heard me say your name. Hold on."

"Hi, Silas, it's Noelle."

"Where are you? Are you coming back? I missed you this morning."

At the worry in his voice, Noelle felt tears sting her eyes. "I missed you too. I had to unexpectedly fly to Boston to help a sick friend. She's feeling better, so I'm able to return to Florida sometime tomorrow."

She heard his sigh, and then he said, "Oh, okay."

"See you tomorrow, Silas," she said, vowing to catch the earliest flight she could, no matter the cost.

As Noelle entered the restaurant, she saw her mother already seated at a table by the window. Observing her mother's eyes light at the sight of her, Noelle filled with gratitude. Her family had always been a warm and welcoming one.

Noelle exchanged hugs with her mother and set her packages down in the empty chair near her. Smiling, she took a seat opposite her mother.

"It's so good to see you!" her mother exclaimed. "Now, tell me why you're here. Does it have something to do with a man?"

Noelle grimaced and said, "Not unless you're talking about a seven-year-old."

Her mother cocked an eyebrow. "What's the story behind that? And is he the reason you're here? The reason you're carrying bags from the children's bookstore?"

Noelle laughed. "One question at a time. Let's order first."

After they'd ordered their Chicken Caesar Salads and were served, Noelle told her mother about Edith, the phone call, and the unexpected flight to Boston.

"This Jake Bellingham, how did you meet him?" her mother asked.

"Through Silas, his son. Silas and I met on the beach and hit it off right away. And then when I met his great-grandmother, I realized she was being physically and medically abused by her caretaker, and I escorted the caretaker out of the house." Noelle held up a hand to stop her mother's protest. "I had to do something for her. She had bruises. It was awful. There was no way I could allow that to continue. And then I helped her grandsons, Jake and Brett Bellingham, find a new caretaker for her. Then I agreed to help Silas with a Christmas project. It's all very complicated," she ended lamely.

Noelle twitched in her seat, well aware of the look her mother was giving her. Jen North expected the best from her children and she didn't like what she was hearing. "It sounds to me like it's more than complicated. And Bellingham? Are you talking about the people who own the Bellingham hotels?"

"Yes. A horrible thing has happened to the family. Brett and Jake's parents were flying together in a small plane that went down over the Rockies. They're still missing and presumed dead. That's why Silas is in Florida at his great-grandmother's house for the school holidays. Jake and his brother have taken control of the hotels as they await word about their parents."

"That's awful. I can't imagine something like that happening in our family."

"I haven't always gotten along with Jake, and neither of us wants more than friendship, but I was very touched by his hiring a jet to bring me to Boston."

Noelle's mother frowned. "I'm worried you might get too caught up in the family. I know you said you're just friends, but Alex hurt you terribly, and either of these men could do that too with their fancy lifestyles and the ability to have anything they want."

Noelle sat quietly. While Jake and Brett had the means to satisfy their every whim, they weren't selfish. In fact, they were generous.

"Well?" her mother said.

"Jake and Brett are nothing like Alex. Don't worry, I have no intention of having a relationship with either of them. Brett is like my brother, and Jake has been very hurt in the past and isn't interested in me at all."

"And what about the little boy?"

"Silas is a darling child, one who's still suffering from the death of his mother over two years ago. He and I connected from the beginning. I promised to help him decorate a Christmas tree in memory of his mother. We're using shells we find along the beach to decorate the tree. It's really a sweet thing for him to do."

"But you'll be leaving him in several weeks," protested Noelle's mother.

"Yes, I've talked to him about that. He needs to understand I'll be back in Boston after the New Year."

"Those women at the New Life community adore you. One of my friends' mother is there, and she speaks highly of you." Her mother reached across the table and squeezed her hand. "You're such a wonderful person, Noelle. I'm anxious for you to find love again, but I don't want you to get hurt, either."

"I know. I'm being careful too. But the trip to Florida has been healthy for me. I've even been experimenting with cooking. Now that I have more time to myself, I'm finding it fun. I'll never be as good as you, but I'm learning."

"Nice," said her mother. "The secret to cooking is to add a touch of love to any dish. Heaven knows I'm not a fancy cook, but my food is tasty. And with you children out on your own, your father and I have changed things up a bit. We eat a little later and lighter."

"I'm taking more time to enjoy things like watching the sunsets. And, Mom, if I didn't have my commitments here, I'd like to live in Florida. In fact, as pretty as it is here with all the decorations, I already miss the palm trees, the water, the sand."

"Do you miss us?" her mother asked, giving her a steady look. Her mother liked her children nearby.

"Of course, but I like it there too."

"Well, I'll be glad to have you back in Boston," her mother announced, signaling the waitress.

"Yes?" The waitress waited for an answer.

"My daughter and I are going to splurge on dessert. Isn't that right, Noelle?"

Laughing, Noelle nodded. Her mother had a sweet tooth and looked for any excuse to satisfy it.

As they were getting ready to leave the restaurant, Noelle's phone rang. She looked at caller ID and turned it off. No way was she going to talk to Jake Bellingham in front of her mother!

Noelle walked Edith down the hall of the main building to her apartment at the New Life Assisted-Living Community.

A crowd quickly gathered around, and questions were thrown at them like colorful confetti.

Laughing, Noelle held up her hand. "Follow us and we'll give you the lowdown on Edith. And, no, I'm not staying for long. I'm flying back to Florida tomorrow."

A sign saying: "Welcome Home, Edith!" was posted on the door to Edith's apartment. Seeing it, Edith placed a hand on her chest. "I can't believe the reception I'm getting."

Noelle gave her a gentle squeeze. "That's because everyone loves you, Edith. Like I do."

Edith smiled even as tears filled her eyes.

Noelle helped her inside and settled her in her favorite chair. Michelle Sanders, the nurse Noelle had chosen to assist Edith hurried over to them. In her forties, a grandmother already, and with an infectious laugh, she was the perfect choice to help Edith through some life changes.

"So glad you're back," Michelle said to Edith, and turned to Noelle. "You're really not going to stay?"

Noelle shook her head. "I can't. It's a long story. A little boy is waiting for my return, and I won't let him down."

"Does this have to do with the man who flew you here in a private jet? The handsome man in that photograph with you?"

A sigh escaped Noelle's lips. "Does everyone know about that?"

Michelle's smile was impish. "Of course. There are no secrets here. Besides, we're all rooting for you to find a decent guy."

"Thanks, but no thanks. I appreciate being on my own without worrying about a man. I've even begun cooking and find I like doing it."

"Oh, you really are serious," said Michelle. "You used to hate cooking."

After the crowd thinned out, Edith remained in her chair while Dorothy, Hazel, and Rose took seats on the couch nearby.

"Okay," Dorothy said to Noelle. "You have a lot to share with us."

Noelle sat in a chair next to Edith. She knew they wouldn't allow her to leave without spilling a story or two about her time in Florida.

With four sets of eyes on her, Noelle began telling them about meeting Silas, their growing friendship, and how, after meeting his great-grandmother she realized she was being abused by her caretaker.

"You threw her out on the spot?" said Dorothy, grinning. "You go, girl!"

"Yes, we can't have that," said Hazel. "It's a lucky thing you were there, Noelle."

Edith leaned forward. "Noelle, dear, we need to know about that young man, Jake Bellingham. You say there's nothing but friendship there, but are you sure?"

Noelle nodded. "He's been very thoughtful about flying me up here to see you, but that's all it is. He's a nice guy with a lot of baggage. Neither of us wants anything more than to be friends. And, honestly, there are times when he drives me crazy."

Rose grinned. "That could be a good thing. My husband, Joe, and I drove each other crazy, but sometimes crazy turns out to be fun, you know?"

"I'm not sure," Noelle said. "He thinks I'm a busybody, bossy nurse who works for him. I told him I'd help his son and his grandmother, but I was doing it for free. Just because he has money, he thinks he can buy my services. I'm not falling for a guy like that. Did that once, remember."

All four heads bobbed up and down.

"Yes, that man was so awful to you," clucked Hazel. "Imagine his leaving you like that."

"It's over and done with," said Edith, giving Hazel a disapproving look. "Time to move on."

"Oh, yes," said Hazel. "Of course."

"Plan B," said Dorothy.

The three other women in the group glanced at Noelle and turned to Dorothy.

"Right," said Dorothy, receiving their private messages. "Give it time, Noelle. Good things will happen for you. I just know it." The four women smiled at Noelle, giving her a sense of unease. They were definitely up to something.

"Ladies, I truly thank you for your concern, but I'm able to take care of myself. The trip to Florida was a wonderful idea, and I've begun to see things in a different way. I really don't need a man in my life. I understand that now."

The expressions of horror on their faces brought a laugh out of Noelle. "Don't look at me like that. It's true."

Edith reached over and patted her hand. "We'll see, my dear. We'll see."

Her friends nodded.

Edith smiled. "Noelle, dear, hadn't you better run along? You told me something about a dinner."

"Oh, yes. My mother has called the family together. Long lost child and all that." Noelle checked her watch and got to her feet. "Let me hug each of you goodbye. I'll see you after the New Year. Until then, you know I'll be thinking of you."

She gave each woman a hug, loving the way they returned it. This is what she needed.

Sitting at the long table that had dominated her parent's large kitchen for years, Noelle realized she also needed this. Loud family gatherings reminded her of what was important in life. And though a man in her life might be nice, it had to be the right person or, as she'd told the women at New Life, she was content to be alone experiencing new things. Watching her parents smile at one another, she wouldn't settle for less.

CHAPTER THIRTEEN

Noelle was sitting in the gate area for her flight to Florida when her cell rang. *Jake Bellingham.*

"Hi, sorry I couldn't get back to you earlier. How are things going with Edith?"

"Fine. She's back at her apartment under careful supervision. But I can't thank you enough for getting me to Boston in a hurry. I would've been distraught if she hadn't survived, and I'd missed saying goodbye." As soon as she said the words, Noelle thought of the dilemma Jake and Brett shared. "I'm sorry ... I didn't think ..."

"It's all right, Noelle. Wonderful news! My parents were found yesterday. They're alive, but seriously injured. The pilot didn't make it, but my mother and father were able to get to a cabin a couple of miles away. It's a miracle I'm still trying to process."

Noelle's heart raced. "That's fabulous! I'm so happy for you! Where are they now?"

"At the University of Colorado Hospital in Denver. I saw them yesterday. Brett is with them now. I'm back in New York, but I'm trying to make it to Florida later today. Do you want to catch a ride back to Florida in the jet?"

"Thanks, but I'm at Logan Airport now. Is there anything I can do to help you and Brett? You must be overwhelmed by the happy news and all that follows."

"It would be great if you could spend extra time with Silas. We're going to fly my parents to Tampa to a rehabilitation center at the hospital so they'll be closer to Nana's house, and

Brett and I can visit them more often. But Silas needs to know someone is there for him."

"Not a problem. I'm anxious to see him anyhow. And, Jake, I'm so very happy your parents are all right. As you said, it is truly a miracle."

"Thanks." Jake's voice quavered, and Noelle knew how grateful he was.

On the flight south, Noelle stared out the window of the plane at the clouds floating above the ground like cottonwood seeds, their shadows covering the fields and homes below in a checkered design. She thought of the miracle of finding Jake's parents alive. Life was full of unexpected moments. For a long time, she'd felt lost and uncertain. The kindness of her friends at New Life had sent her to Florida where she was discovering a fresh outlook on life. She didn't know what the future held, but whatever it was, she would embrace it.

And later, as the hired driver drew his car into the driveway of Seashell Cottage, Noelle's heart leapt with joy. It felt so good to be back among palm trees and sandy beaches. Better yet, she'd see Silas and help him continue his search for the tree decorations that meant so much to him.

She paid the driver and then carried her suitcase to the front door. On the front porch, she stood a moment and inhaled the salty air, feeling its freshness enter her lungs. It hardly seemed possible that so much had happened in the three days since she'd been here. Opening the door, she stepped inside. Everything was just as she left it. In the kitchen, the dishes had been hastily rinsed and stacked in the sink, the food put away. But the table was still set with the placemats she'd used, and the hibiscus blossom in a container placed in the center of the table had long since wilted into a sad, dried clump.

Noelle unpacked her suitcase, straightened the kitchen, and added several items to the grocery list she now kept on the counter. Satisfied things were in order, she called Dora to tell her she was on her way to see Silas.

"Lots of excitement here, but I think it's been confusing to Silas. His grandparents are alive, but his mother is still dead. That kind of thing."

"Oh? Thanks for telling me. I'll keep it in mind."

Noelle picked up one of the art projects she'd purchased and headed down the beach. She'd found it was easier to talk to Silas when he was busy doing something.

As she walked along the sand, Noelle thought back to the first time she'd seen Silas. With his red hair and freckles he was still the cutest boy ever. He'd confided that he didn't like his hair, but she'd convinced him for a while that it was her favorite color. In any case, with his Bellingham features and healthy physique, he was destined to be a handsome man.

From a distance she saw Duke running toward her with Silas at his heels. Her heart swelled with affection, and she hurried forward to meet them.

"Noelle! You're here!" cried Silas running into her open arms.

"Yes, my sick friend is going to be all right. By the time I leave Florida, she'll be all better."

"Poppy and Gran are almost healed," Silas announced. "They came from the mountains. Dad says it's a miracle. Uncle Brett says so too."

"Ah, yes. It's a wonderful thing. Miracles sometimes happen, you know."

Silas gave her a steady look and shook his head. "I don't think so. Mom's not here."

"No, she's not. I'm sorry. I know it makes you sad."

"Yes," said Silas solemnly.

Noelle held up the brightly-colored bag she was carrying. "I've got a new project for us. Let's get started on it, and then tomorrow morning we'll look for more shells."

As they walked toward Althea's house, Gracie left a group on the beach and hurried over to them. "Hi, Thilath. Are you looking for thellth?"

"Not right now," he answered. "We're going to do a project."

"We'll look for some shells in the morning," said Noelle. "Maybe, if you're out on the beach at the same time, we can look for them together. Okay, Silas?"

Silas studied Noelle and turned to Gracie. "Okay."

The smile that creased Gracie's face was touching to see. "Okay." She turned and ran back to her family.

"Thank you, Silas. That was very nice of you," Noelle said.

He shrugged. "I know."

Smiling, Noelle ruffled his hair.

They entered Althea's house together. "Wait just a moment," Noelle said. "I need to speak to your Nana."

The minute Noelle entered Althea's room, she noticed a difference. Althea was not asleep or slumped in a chair. She was standing at the window looking out at the water.

"So beautiful," Althea murmured. "I'd forgotten what it was like to simply watch the waves roll in and out."

Noelle came up beside her. "Yes, it *is* beautiful. And how are you?"

Althea smiled. "My boy is okay."

"Yes, I heard that both Willis and Stephanie are going to be fine. I'm so happy for you."

Althea's smile widened. "Jacob will be so happy to hear that. I must remember to tell him."

"Of course. He'll be happy too," Noelle responded, well

aware that Jacob had been dead for many years.

Noelle left Althea and went into the kitchen to find Silas. He was sitting at the kitchen table with the art project opened in front of him.

"I like puzzles. Now I can make my own," he said.

"Yes. You make a drawing on the cardboard, and then we'll cut it in different pieces, following the sample they've given you."

"What shall I draw?" Silas asked.

"Anything you want," Noelle said. "Take your time. I need to talk to Dora."

Once Silas was engaged in the activity, Noelle and Dora stepped outside the kitchen away from the back entrance.

"Jake asked me to spend some extra time with Silas, and I'm concerned about what you told me. Is there something special I should know regarding his confusion over his grandparents' surviving?"

"He's seen how emotional his father and uncle are, and he's worried about them. He understands they're really happy over their parents' survival, but he wants the same thing to happen to his mother. He's gone from thinking his grandparents were dead to suddenly having them alive. He's had a couple of bad dreams."

"Okay. This is your night off. If Jake doesn't make it home and I have to sleep over, I'll try to be aware of that. Thanks for telling me."

Dora placed a hand on Noelle's shoulder. "Silas has taken quite a fancy to you. He told me he wants you to be his new mother. I told him I didn't think that was possible. I didn't know what else to say."

"That's the truth. Jake and I are only friends. It's not possible to be more than that for so many reasons. I have my life in Boston, and I'm about to embark on some new things—

cooking, travel, and other activities I've been putting off."

"Good for you. We don't want to allow Silas to get hurt by wishes that can't come true."

"Exactly," agreed Noelle, wondering why a pang of disappointment pinched her insides.

When Jake called to let Noelle know that he'd be late getting home, Noelle informed Dora and left Althea's house to go to the cottage to pack her overnight bag. If keeping Dora meant she'd have to stay the night a couple of days a week, it was worth it. Dora was a prize they all loved. Althea never looked happier and seemed much more alert without the abundance of medications she'd previously been given. Dora also supervised the house cleaners during the days they were there and continued to cook delicious meals.

As she packed her things, Noelle thought of the days ahead with Jake's parents and added a skirt and blouse to the suitcase on top of her jeans and sweater.

Back at Althea's house, she bid Dora goodbye and quickly settled into Dora's room behind the kitchen. Clean sheets had been put on the bed and fresh towels hung in the bathroom for her. Dora was so thoughtful that way.

Even more thoughtful was the beautiful casserole Dora had put together for their meal. Later, as she served it, Noelle made careful note of the ingredients for the chicken and noodle meal and decided to try it on a smaller scale for herself.

Noelle helped Althea get ready for bed, and made sure Silas had a bath and brushed his teeth before she sat and read a book with him.

With Silas asleep, she went downstairs. Noting the late hour, she brushed her teeth and rubbed skin cream on her face. As she prepared to pull on her pajamas, she heard a car pull into the driveway.

She hurried to the back window and peered out. Jake was climbing out of a limo.

Noelle turned on the outdoor lights to greet him.

He entered the kitchen, saw her, and smiled. "Hi! Glad to see you! I guess Dora is off tonight."

"Yes. A well-deserved break for her. Can I get you anything? Coffee? A drink?"

"How about sharing a glass of wine with me? I haven't had a moment to celebrate my parents' return with anyone."

Understanding his need to talk, she nodded. "That sounds nice. We can sit in the living room where no one will hear us. Both Althea and Silas are sound asleep. Althea seemed so happy to know about 'her boy,' your father." She smiled. "She can't wait to tell Jacob."

He looked startled and then nodded. "Right. In her mind, he's still alive. Sad."

"Yes, it's hard to see the disease progressing. It's awful for the family and sometimes terrifying for the patient."

Jake let out a sigh. "Well, tonight we have something to celebrate. Though they're both battered and bruised, they're going to be all right. Dad always kept himself in shape, and that's what saved his life and my mother's. He has a broken leg, a few broken ribs, and a broken wrist, and yet he half-carried my mother more than two miles to a cabin hidden away in the woods. The authorities don't know how he managed to find the cabin, much less get them there. He's a real hero." Jake's face flushed with emotion. "He's always been a hero to me. They both have. My mother suffered cuts to her face and her head and sprained both ankles. They helped each other to survive. I'm told the cold was a help to them, that if it had been hot and buggy, it would have made things even more difficult. My mother packed her ankles with snow, melted the snow for water, and used it for their survival. There was food in the cabin, but not much. Apparently, she made the food last by adding water and making it into thin soups."

Noelle reached out and touched his arm. "You must be so proud of them. I'm delighted for you that they survived."

"Me too. I wish the pilot could have made it. He died on impact."

Noelle gathered two glasses while Jake retrieved a bottle of wine from the special cooler in the pantry.

After the bottle had been opened and the wine poured, Jake lifted his glass. "Here's to happy endings."

"And miracles," Noelle said, tapping his glass with hers.

They went into the living room and sat down at either end of the couch.

Following a few moments of quiet, Jake turned to her. "Thank you for being such a good friend to the family. We're still searching for a night nurse, but right now Silas needs you."

"I know how busy you are with everything, but sometime, sooner rather than later, we need to talk about him. He's confused and, I suspect, frustrated by the fact that his grandparents have seemingly come back to life and his mother hasn't."

"Really? I'll talk to him about it. These last couple of months have been hard on all of us." He ran a hand across the hair at the back of his head. "Poor guy. I'm going to set up an appointment for him with a psychologist I've heard about in Miami."

"I think that's a wise idea."

Jake stared into the distance and then faced her. "You know, Claire and I never talked like this, searching for ways to make our marriage work. After a while, neither one of us cared, and then she found someone else."

"It's smart to talk things out."

"You really have a way with people, don't you?" Jake gave her smile. "Old and young."

She arched an eyebrow at him. "Not always. Some people have called me bossy, among other things."

Jake laughed. "Guess Brett and I were a little overwhelmed by someone coming into the house and taking charge. We're usually the ones in charge."

"Yes, I know. It's a good thing you're used to it and can make quick decisions like hiring a jet to take me to Boston. The ladies at New Life were so impressed. Me too."

He reached over and clasped her hand. "I was happy to do it." He glanced at his empty wine glass. "Care for another?"

Noelle shook her head. "No thanks. I've had enough." She got to her feet. "I'd better head into bed."

He rose and faced her. "Someday a lucky man will have you by his side." He bent down and kissed her cheek. "Good night, Noelle."

With her cheek on fire, Noelle could only manage a nod and a fluttering of her fingers in a little wave to him. More than the softness of his lips on her skin, the look of desire in his eyes had shaken her to the core.

CHAPTER FOURTEEN

The next morning as she was zipping up the back of the casual dress Althea had chosen to wear, Jake knocked on the door. "I need to ask you for another favor. I just finished talking to Dr. Heard in Miami. He can see Silas late this afternoon. Will you please come with us? After listening to my description about what was going on, he thought it was a smart idea. Dora will come in a little early."

"And we'll return tonight?"

"If you don't mind, I thought we'd stay the night and return tomorrow around noon. That will give me a chance to take care of a business meeting Brett was supposed to run. Are you okay with that?"

"I'm fine with it as long as I don't have to deal with Liz Connors and her online gossip column."

"Fair enough. Don't worry, I'll see that you won't have to." His grin was sly.

She shot him a suspicious look. "What are you going to do?"

"You'll see." He winked at her. "Bring that nice dress of yours."

Her nerves went on high alert. He'd looked exactly like his impish brother. He must be up to no good.

The ride to Miami was relaxing. Jake drove fast but demonstrated easy control of the car. Silas was once again content to play games on his iPad while Noelle enjoyed reading a book on her iPad.

When they got to the hotel and were escorted inside, Noelle felt more comfortable with the attention. She felt the smile on her face as she watched Silas solemnly shake hands with the hotel manager. Whether he knew it or not, Silas was being prepared one day to become part of the family hotel business.

After they were settled in one of the luxury suites, Jake told Silas about the appointment with Dr. Heard.

"You're coming with me?" Silas asked, giving him a worried look.

Jake nodded. "Yes, I'll be there, and Noelle too."

Silas moved closer to her and gazed up at her uncertainly.

"There's nothing to be worried about," she told him. "It's just a chance to talk things over with a very kind man. He'll probably want to ask us all a lot of questions."

"Okay," said Silas.

Jake gave her a grateful look. "We'll take a limo there."

Dr. Jerold Heard was a short, bald man whose fringe of white hair on his head and twinkling blue eyes made Noelle think of Santa Claus. He spoke in a quiet voice and studied them openly as introductions were made.

"Well, young lad, I'm always happy to meet someone who likes seashells. Your father told me you have a book about them."

Silas's face brightened. "You like seashells too? Noelle and I are finding lots of them." He looked at Noelle and then said to Dr. Heard, "I can't tell you more. It's a secret between Noelle and me."

Dr. Heard glanced at Noelle and then nodded to Silas. "Some secrets are good. Others aren't. But this sounds like a good one." He straightened. "Why don't all three of you come into my office while we talk briefly. Then I'll speak individually with Jake and then Silas. Is everyone okay with this?"

Noelle nodded along with Jake. "I know it's unusual to have me present in a situation like this because I'm not family."

Silas frowned at her. "Noelle saved me from Mrs. Wicked," he announced to Dr. Heard.

Only the slightest lift of his eyebrows indicated Dr. Heard's surprise. "Mrs. Wicked, huh?"

"He means Mrs. Wickstrom, the caretaker I discovered abusing his great-grandmother," Noelle quickly said.

Dr. Heard's forehead smoothed out. "I see."

"Noelle has saved our family in other ways by helping out with Silas and my grandmother," Jake said.

Dr. Heard studied her. "Mmm."

He waved them into his office, and after they'd taken seats, he said, "I understand you, Noelle, are here in Florida for a holiday vacation. Any intention of staying on?"

She shook her head. "No, I'm the health director at the New Life Assisted-Living Community west of Boston."

He turned to Silas. "You and Noelle have become great friends in a very short time. Do you understand she'll be leaving Florida after the holidays?"

Silas took a deep breath and said softly, "I want Noelle to be my new mother."

"Oh, honey, no ..." Noelle uttered at the same time Jake said, "Sorry, buddy."

In the awkward silence that followed, Dr. Heard said, "It's clear to me that it's not going to happen. Silas and I will work on that."

"Do you need me to answer any further questions?" Noelle asked him, unable to stop the heat flooding her cheeks.

"No, I don't think so. Perhaps later, you and I can discuss some strategies for handling this situation and others. Why don't you and Silas sit in the waiting room while I talk privately with Jake."

Relieved, Noelle rose to her feet. "C'mon, Silas. Let's take a little break." She held out her hand, and he took it.

In the waiting room, they sat together on the only couch. Silas bowed his head and when he lifted it there were tears in his eyes. "Why can't you stay in Florida?"

"Because I have a family and a job at home in Boston." she said quietly. She took her cell phone from her purse. "Look! I'll show you some pictures of the place where I work and some of the people who live there."

Noelle aimed her phone at Silas. "Smile. We'll send those women your photograph so they have an idea of what a handsome young man you are. They already know that you're a special friend of mine."

He hammed it up with a funny face, but anyone could see from the photograph how adorable Silas was. Noelle sent the photo to each of the so-called Three Musketeers Plus One.

"There, now let me show you their pictures." As she showed Silas the photographs, she talked about each of the women.

"What do you think?" Noelle asked.

"They're awfully old," said Silas. "Well, maybe not as old as Nana. Dad said she was as old as 'Thusla."

"Methuselah?" Noelle laughed softly. "That's very, very old."

"I know," said Silas.

Jake appeared. "Your turn, Silas. Remember, you can tell Dr. Heard anything you want. Have fun." He walked Silas inside Dr. Heard's office and returned alone.

"How did it go?" Noelle asked.

Jake sighed. "It's good that we came. He's going to help

both Silas and me."

Noelle remained quiet as he got up and stared out the window. He turned back to her. "Considering all that's happening with my parents, he's agreed to meet with Silas tomorrow morning so he has a better understanding of everything including losing you."

She clasped a hand to her chest. "I'm sorry, but I've always said I have to get back to Boston."

"I understand." He studied her a moment and turned to the window.

Again, Noelle remained quiet. She didn't know what Jake and Dr. Heard had discussed, but Jake seemed very subdued.

A while later, Silas emerged from Dr. Heard's office smiling and holding a brown, soft, stuffed dog. He held it up for them to see. "This is King."

"What a nice dog," said Noelle.

"May I see you for a moment?" Dr. Heard asked her.

"Sure," Noelle said automatically, though she wondered why he'd want to speak to her alone.

She entered his office and took a seat in a leather chair opposite him.

"I felt I needed to let you know not only how fond Silas is of you, but how much he trusts you. This secret project of yours—is it something I should know about? I'm working with Silas on being free to say anything he wants, but even with all my probing skills, he's remained firm in keeping the secret he shares with you."

Noelle grinned. "He almost spilled the beans once. I'm glad to see he's keeping his word. It's an idea I developed as a means for him to celebrate Christmas in a unique way. He wanted to decorate a Christmas tree because he remembers how much his mother loved them. We are now collecting seashells to hang on the tree as a special Florida Christmas."

"A nice idea," commented Dr. Heard.

"After hearing about some of his concerns, I've thought that maybe we can use those decorations to make wishes or write messages to remember this time. We'd write them on small pieces of paper and either glue them where we can or attach them somehow. I've done something similar with residents of New Life, where I work. What do you think?"

Dr. Heard was quiet and then nodded. "That's another great idea, and if there's any information you think would be helpful to me, will you please relay it to me privately?"

"Yes, of course. I have a feeling Silas will share a lot of the things he's worrying about, but, of course, if he asks me not to tell or I sense he doesn't want me to say anything about it, I won't. I can't break the trust between us."

"Absolutely. Though you're not his doctor, you're a most trusted friend. The dog can be used as a prompt when you see him struggling to say something. I find it a great means of allowing young patients a safe way to speak." He smiled. "The dog, of course, can't reprimand, or scold, or represent any fear to the one speaking to it."

"Mmm. I'll have to remember that for some of my people at New Life."

"Thank you. You certainly have done a nice job with Silas so far. He adores you, which might be a helpful reason for him to talk to me after you're gone."

"I'll work with you on that," Noelle said.

Dr. Heard got to his feet, ending their discussion.

On the trip back to the hotel, it was quiet in the limo. Noelle brushed away the guilt she felt knowing how hurt Silas would be by her leaving to go back home.

Later, Noelle sat by the hotel's swimming pool watching

Silas play and swim in the water. It had been an emotional day, and she was tired.

Jake approached her. "I've arranged for a babysitter to stay with Silas. He already knows I'd planned to do it, and it's okay with him. Besides, it's been a long day and I have a feeling he'll drop off to sleep pretty early."

"All right," Noelle said, wondering what he was up to.

His smile sent a sparkle to his gray eyes. "I'll pick you up at the suite at seven o'clock for dinner."

"But ..."

Jake held up a hand to stop her. "It won't be in the hotel restaurant, so you won't have to deal with Liz."

She watched Jake walk away and observed the looks of interest on the faces of the women sitting poolside as he strode by. Some even turned to study her. She knew she was no match for a lot of the young models who loved South Beach and enhanced the beaches and pools with their long-legged beauty. But Jake seemed not to have noticed.

Noelle turned away from the prying eyes. The last thing she wanted was another blurb in any online society column associating her with Jake. It might end up hurting Silas. And what a stir it would cause with the women at New Life. They'd never stop nagging her about it.

"Hey, Noelle! Look!" Silas waved to her from the pool and then did his best to do a somersault.

When his face emerged from the water, he gave her a questioning look.

"Great!" Noelle said.

The smile that crossed Silas's face looked so similar to Jake's that her breath caught. The Bellingham men, all three of them, were handsome.

###

As Jake had predicted, Silas had no problem with getting into his pajamas a little early. He'd played in the pool until he was so tired he announced he wanted to go back to the room. And he loved the idea of ordering room service and being waited on.

Noelle noticed with interest that King, Silas's new stuffed dog, stayed in his lap as he ate.

After his meal, Silas was content to sit on the couch watching television. Noelle used that time to shower and dress for the evening. As Jake had suggested, she wore the black dress that he'd seen on her earlier. It looked even better with her skin glowing from the sun. She rolled mascara on her eyelashes and added eyeshadow to her eyelids. Standing back, she assessed herself. "As good as it gets," Noelle said, turning away from the image she knew was not perfect.

When she stepped into the living room, Silas looked up at her and smiled. "You look beautiful, Noelle."

Feeling a surge of tenderness for him, Noelle went over to the couch and sat down beside him. "Thank you, Silas. That's a nice thing to say to a woman."

He nodded. "I know."

She laughed, wondering how often he'd heard it said.

"Noelle? King wants you to give Silas a kiss."

Blinking back the tears that stung her eyes, she said, "Come here, Silas."

She pulled him into her lap and hugged him to her. She kissed his cheek and said softly, "What else does King want Noelle to know?"

"He wants me to tell you that I'm going to find the best, biggest Christmas star ever just for you."

"That would be nice," Noelle said. "But decorating the tree with you is a wonderful gift all by itself."

Silas looked up at her. "Better than a Christmas star?"

"Yes. You and me surprising the family with a pretty tree." Silas snuggled closer to her.

Jake entered the room. "So, this is how you two spend time when I'm away working," he said, beaming as he approached them.

Silas jumped off Noelle's lap and ran over to him. "Noelle and I are going to make the prettiest Christmas tree ever!"

Jake picked up Silas and hugged him. "I'm sure it will be. The two of you are a fantastic team."

Noelle got to her feet. "Give me a minute, and I'll be ready to go." In her room she sat on her bed, shaken. For a brief second, she'd had the image of the three of them together like this in the future. She told herself it was her imagination, that this time of year did funny things with her mind and her emotions.

"You ready?" Jake called through the door.

"Just a minute more." She got to her feet, brushed off her dress, and took a deep breath. Moments like that were exactly why she'd decided not to celebrate the Christmas holidays. Shattered dreams, unfulfilled wishes, foolish thoughts plagued her during this time.

When she emerged, Silas rushed over to her. "You look beautiful again, Noelle."

"Again?" said Jake, glancing at her with a questioning look.

She laughed. "He said that earlier and I told him it was a nice thing to say to a woman."

Jake nodded. "I get it." He patted Silas on the back. "Way to go, son."

"I know," said Silas with amusing confidence.

Jake and Noelle smiled at one another.

The doorbell to the suite rang, and Silas raced to answer it.

A gray-haired woman stood in the doorway.

Jake hurried over to her. "You must be Mrs. Murphy, one

of the hotel's babysitters. I'm glad to meet you. All the reports I've read about you are excellent."

"Yes, sir." She gave a tiny bob of her head. "I'm happy to be of service."

"Are you going to read me a story?" Silas asked her.

Mrs. Murphy smiled. "I love reading stories."

"King likes them too." He held up the stuffed dog. "This is King. He loves books about Captain Underpants. I have a big dog at home. His name is Duke. He likes those books too."

"Well, then that's what we'll read," Mrs. Murphy said agreeably.

"I imagine Silas will fade fast. It's been a busy day," said Jake. He turned and hugged Silas. "Have fun and behave for Mrs. Murphy."

"I know," said Silas, saying it this time with impatience.

"See you in the morning," said Noelle, giving him a quick hug, and then obliging Silas's wishes, hugged the stuffed dog Silas held up to her.

"Later, alligator," Silas said, bringing a smile to her face.

Jake led her out of the suite, down the corridor, and into the elevator.

"Where are we going?" Noelle asked.

Jake grinned and pushed a button on the elevator's panel. "You'll see."

"Wait!" said Noelle. "We're going up."

"Exactly. I thought we might have dinner in the Presidential Suite. It's not in use."

Noelle's lips curved. "It sounds lovely. I'm ready for a relaxing evening."

"Me too."

CHAPTER FIFTEEN

On the top floor of the hotel, Noelle stepped off the elevator into a reception area outside wide double doors. An arrangement of fresh flowers sat on a long, narrow table that stood against the wall on one side of the doors. An upholstered bench of equal length sat on the other side. Admiring the setting, Noelle could hardly wait to see the interior.

Jake knocked on the door.

A man dressed in a butler's uniform opened it and smiled at them. "Good evening, Mr. Bellingham. Welcome to our Presidential Suite. I hope you and your lady will have a pleasant evening here."

"Thank you. I'm sure we will. I appreciate your help."

The butler made a small bow. "Yes, sir. We've done everything as ordered." He stepped away and held the door for them, indicating for them to enter.

Jake held back and then followed Noelle inside.

She stopped a moment to appreciate the setting. The large, green Oriental rug covering most of the off-white carpet in the living area served as the foundation of the color scheme of green, white, and hibiscus pink. Green-and-white-striped fabric covered two of the overstuffed chairs. A floral print with a green background featured flowers in white, pink, and orange. Two white-leather couches faced each other, accented with pink pillows and others covered in a pink, white, and green plaid. A glossy-white grand piano filled the far corner of the room. Noelle felt as if she were in a lovely, tropical garden.

Jake led her to a small room off the living room.

"Thought we'd have a drink here in the library."

"Sounds lovely," Noelle said, gazing at the white shelves along the interior wall loaded with books. The two green loveseats in front of the shelves were inviting.

She sat in one of them and looked around while Jake signaled the butler that they were ready for their drinks. She loved the idea of having some time to relax without thinking about cooking a meal for herself or cleaning up afterward.

Jake smiled as he sat on the loveseat across from her. "I thought you might enjoy a nice evening without worrying about Liz or anyone else making trouble for us."

"I appreciate it. The last week has been hectic and challenging. I can't imagine what you've gone through with all the emotions of thinking you'd lost your parents and then finding them alive."

"It was a huge shock when we got the news they'd survived, but oh, so wonderful. Brett and I, along with the authorities, had pretty much given up the idea that they could've made it out of there alive. Now, we have to make sure they heal well and that the business keeps running smoothly."

"Will your father take over again?"

Jake shook his head. "I don't think so. He was thinking of retiring soon, and from what he indicated when I last spoke to him, both he and my mother intend to spend the rest of their lives catching up on things they've missed doing in the past."

"So, you and Brett will continue," Noelle said as the butler offered her a flute of champagne.

"Yes. That's the plan." Jake accepted champagne, and after the butler left, he lifted his flute in a toast to her. "Here's to health and happiness!"

"Oh, yes! Health and happiness. Who could ask for more?" She held up her glass and smiled at him.

They each took a sip of the bubbly white wine and let out sighs of contentment.

"This is delicious," said Noelle.

"Hold on. The best is yet to come."

The butler walked in with a tray and set it down on a small coffee table in front of her. A small crystal container of caviar, toast points on a plate, chopped hard-boiled eggs, lemon wedges, crème fraiche, and slivered red onion in side dishes sat atop the tray's surface. Noelle clasped her hands together. "Oh my! You know how much I love caviar! But, Jake, you didn't need to do something like this."

He grinned. "I wanted to thank you for coming with Silas and me to Dr. Heard's office. I think the days leading up to Christmas may give him the chance to open up about what's bothering him."

"I hope so. He's such a fine boy." Lifting a piece of toast, she scooped a small spoonful of caviar on top and added a tiny bit of crème fraiche. She slipped it into her mouth and closed her eyes. It tasted fabulous.

"I'm glad you're enjoying the caviar," said Jake.

She opened her eyes and smiled at him. "It's divine."

He studied her. "You know when you befriended Silas and shook things up at Nana's house, I thought you might be after money or some other favor from the family."

"And now?"

His look was sheepish. "Now I know better."

"My ex-fiancé thought he could have anything he wanted by just paying for it. It's something I've never liked. However, it worked for him because the woman he ended up marrying, his old girlfriend, loves flaunting all the material things he's given her. And to be totally honest, he does too."

"Ah, I see now why you took issue when I offered you money."

"How about you? You have all these privileges, places like this you can use."

Jake chuckled. "Believe me, this is an exception to my normal lifestyle. Hotel work is constant, competitive, and 24/7. I enjoy what I have, but all the material things are not what motivates me. I want to make our hotels the best they can be by providing our guests with a positive experience. That takes ongoing oversight and careful management of financials. If the Bellingham name is attached to it, I want it to be right."

"Do you want to grow and add more hotels? Brett mentioned a hotel in Paris."

"Definitely not. That was Dad's idea. After dealing with the hotel in London, Brett and I are content with what we have. We don't want to get sucked into working constantly. We want time for our personal lives too." He stirred in his seat. "I know it goes against some business practices, but after thinking we'd lost both parents, it was an easy decision for Brett and me to make. Our parents worked all the time."

"I like that you are happy with what you have," said Noelle, feeling genuine respect for him.

"After speaking to Dr. Heard about Silas, I feel it's the right position to take," he continued.

"Me too. His face lights up when he talks about you."

Jake's cheeks flushed with pleasure. "Really?"

"Oh, yes."

After sharing more caviar and sipping the champagne, Jake checked his watch. "I didn't realize it was so late. Shall we go into dinner?"

"Sure." Noelle didn't know what he had planned for their meal, but if it was anything like the appetizer, it was bound to be fantastic.

Jake ushered her into the dining room. A long, mahogany

table that could seat twelve was in the center of the room. A large sideboard covered a portion of the pale-pink interior wall.

"We're together at one end. As you can see, the table is used for both dining and as a conference table." Two place settings were established at the end of the table closest to the wall of windows overlooking the beach and the ocean beyond it.

Noelle walked over to the windows and stared out at the scene below. The sun had long since set but lights glittered like stars from the buildings lining the shore. Light from the moon laid a path across the water, like the yellow-brick road in Dorothy's story.

Jake came up behind her. "Seeing a moonlit path like that always makes me wonder what or who is at the exact opposite spot on the far shores."

She liked the idea of sharing similar thoughts and smiled. "Me too."

The butler appeared behind them. "Dinner service is ready any time, sir."

Jake turned around. "Guess it's not fair to the chef to keep it waiting. You may go ahead and tell him. And please pour us each a glass of the decanted wine."

"Madame?" Jake playfully held out an arm for her to take.

Going along with him, she took it and allowed him to lead her to her chair at the table.

A man in a white chef's coat soon entered the room wheeling a cart holding two covered plates. "I think you'll find this meal quite suitable," he announced, placing a plate of food in front of Noelle and then Jake. With a flourish, he lifted the silver covers from the plates.

"Mmm. It smells and looks delicious," said Noelle, inhaling the aroma of lemon, garlic, and a host of other smells.

"Beef Wellington, lemon and garlic roasted potatoes, and

French green beans," the chef announced with pride. "A crisp romaine salad will follow."

"Thank you so much," said Jake. "It's cooked beautifully."

Alone in the room, they dug into their food.

"The crust on the Wellington is delightful, so crisp," said Noelle, wondering if the day would come when she would dare to try a recipe as fancy as this.

"I specifically ordered this meal because the next occupant of this suite has requested a private dinner, and I wanted to make sure this would do nicely for him."

"Oh, he'll be happy," said Noelle, taking another taste of the rare roast tenderloin.

Jake looked at her and smiled. "Please don't be offended, but I usually don't see women enjoying their food like you do."

"What's better than an excellent meal? I don't eat huge portions, but I want what I eat to be tasty. Otherwise, why bother?" As she said the words she understood her enjoyment this evening came from sharing the meal with him.

Jake's smile crinkled the skin at the corner of his eyes. He shook his head. "You are one of a kind, Noelle North."

She shrugged. "I am who I am." Noelle realized how much good this trip had done for her. Others might have been led to believe from all the gossip that she was such a horrible person that Alex had left her at the church. At least this man appreciated her for who she was.

When prompted, Jake told stories of funny happenings at the hotels. Soon, they were laughing.

As they finished their main course and began on the salad course, Jake set down his fork and gazed at her. "I can't remember when I've had such a relaxing evening. Thank you, Noelle."

"You can ask me to eat this kind of food with you anytime," she joked.

Jake's expression grew serious. "I know you don't want any serious relationships right now, but couldn't we share some meals now and then? I've thought of a recipe I'd like to try with you."

"That might be fun. You could cook at the cottage and show me what you're doing," Noelle said.

"Sounds great," Jake said. "It may be a last-minute thing, but as soon as I can arrange some time, we'll do it. You'll be going back to Boston, and I might as well teach you as much as I can in the weeks we have left."

Warmth flooded Noelle's body and crept to her cheeks. The thought of spending more time with Jake was even more appealing than the food he promised her.

Dessert was a slice of Crème Brûlée Cheesecake and a cup of decaf coffee.

Mentally counting the number of laps she would have to swim in the pool tomorrow to burn off the calories, Noelle sighed with satisfaction. "What a fabulous meal!"

"I don't think any guests could complain about a meal like that," said Jake. He helped Noelle out of her chair and walked her over to the window. "A beautiful night."

"Yes," she agreed. "It's lovely."

He turned to her. "I really like you, you know."

"It's been a wonderful evening and I've enjoyed getting to know you better."

They smiled at each other. Jake leaned toward her and ... and the butler entered the room, shattering the moment. "Sorry, sir, I thought you and your lady had left."

"Not a problem," Jake said, but there was a note of disappointment in his voice.

The next morning, as Jake and Silas were getting ready to

leave for Dr. Heard's office, Jake turned to her.

"Do me a favor, will you? Check out the gift and clothing shops here and tell me what you think."

"I've hoped to be able to do just that," she said, pleased he cared about her opinion.

As they headed to the door, Silas, holding King, said, "Later, alligator."

She laughed. "After a while, crocodile."

Silas burst into laughter. "'Bye, crocodile."

Noelle still had a smile on her face as she prepared to do a little scout work in the shops.

A while later, Noelle decided the gift shop, the men's shop, and the evening-wear store were fine as they were, nothing special, but fine. Her favorite store was a shop of women's clothing. Seaside Boutique carried the kind of clothes she liked—casual but with a subtle, more upscale difference. The sales clerk was genuinely friendly and eagerly showed her around. Noelle left with a sundress she'd found on sale.

Noelle was overwhelmed by the jewelry store. It was filled with dazzling, sparkling, glittering jewels. She browsed throughout it, taking in everything. The pleasant clerk answered her questions about prices, stones, and suggested wear. She left the store certain Jake would be pleased to know he had such a knowledgeable person working there.

When Jake and Silas returned to the suite, Noelle handed him a sheet of paper with her notes on the stores.

He studied it. "Great job! This is the kind of information I'm looking for." He looked up at her with a grin. "Guess I'll have to bring all the food to our cooking sessions. I know you won't let me pay you."

She laughed. "I'll think of the most expensive items I can."

"Is Dad cooking?" Silas asked, breaking into their teasing banter.

"He's going to teach me some things," Noelle said. When she noticed the devilish grin that crossed Jake's face and realized what he might be thinking, she covered her mouth with her fingertips.

"Are we going home now?" Silas asked. "King told me he wants to see Duke."

Jake turned to him. "You want to see Duke? Okay, let's get all your things together. Last time, we almost left your iPad behind."

Noelle went to her room to get her overnight bag. She'd packed earlier but hadn't placed her new sundress inside.

As she was zipping her bag, Jake came to the door. "I'll take it down. It's a busy time for check-outs, and I don't want to interrupt the staff."

She handed it over to him. "How did the appointment with Silas go?"

"It went well." Jake hesitated and then blurted out, "Dr. Heard is helping me to trust relationships again." He swallowed hard and gave a helpless shrug of his shoulders. "I don't know why I told you that. Probably too much information."

"No, I think it's nice," Noelle said, realizing how embarrassed he was. The man who so easily handled a tough business was not so tough himself.

CHAPTER SIXTEEN

On the way back to Althea's house, Jake received a call from Brett in Colorado telling him that their parents were being flown out on a private jet later that week. The doctors wanted to be sure the trauma to their bodies was under control before allowing them to fly to Florida.

Noelle listened to the news through the bluetooth phone connection and watched Jake's expression grow tender. "You tell Mom and Dad I'm thinking of them. I'll be there to help them with the flight home."

"Right. I'm about to leave for New York for the investors' conference taking place at the hotel."

"Thanks. I've checked on things at South Beach and have some suggestions for the retail section. Noelle did a little survey for me this morning."

"Noelle? Is she there with you now?"

Jake signaled her to answer.

"Hi, Brett. I came over to Miami to go to Silas's doctor's appointment."

"You owe me a dinner, you know."

Noelle laughed. "We'll see."

"You might have to get in line, bro," Jake said. "I'm teaching Noelle how to cook a few of my favorite dishes."

"You think bossy lady is going to allow you to tell her how to do something?" Brett said.

Noelle heard the laughter in his voice but had to respond. "By the time I cook dinner for you, I'll be an even better cook than Jake."

"I knew it! Can't wait. Gotta go. Jake, I'll call you later."

After the call ended, Jake turned to her. "This cooking challenge ... you know I'm going to win. Right?"

"Maybe," she responded, suddenly excited about the idea of working at a stove.

After she unpacked at the cottage, Noelle got into her car and hurried down to the mall to find some cookbooks. Instead of reading her beloved romance novels, she was going to read up on cooking tips, rules, and procedures. Now that Jake had challenged her, she wanted to learn everything she could about cooking.

As she entered the cottage, her cell rang. She set down her packages on the kitchen table and checked caller ID. *Martin Vogel.* Frowning, she clicked on the call. "Hello?"

"Is this Noelle North?"

"Yes. Who is this?"

"Hi, I'm Martin Vogel, Hazel Vogel's great-nephew."

Noelle's heart thumped in her chest. "Oh, my word! Has something happened to Hazel?"

"Not at all. I'm merely doing her a favor by calling you. I've owed her a favor for some time." He cleared his throat. "I would like to ask you out for dinner. Perhaps this Friday evening?"

"I don't know ..."

"Please, this is very important to my aunt. And from her description of you, I'd really like to meet you."

"You're talking about a blind date? Whatever is she doing?"

"It's not just her. She and her friends called me. I'm apparently their Plan B."

"Oh my God!" Noelle couldn't help the laugh that bubbled out of her in great guffaws. "You poor guy! I don't know what she did for you that you'd owe her this, but I'll go along with them. They'd be so disappointed if I didn't."

"So, we'll have dinner on Friday?" The relief in Marty's voice was almost comical. "What do you say I pick you up at seven o'clock?"

"Sounds fine. And, Marty, don't worry. It'll simply be dinner."

Noelle clicked off the call and sat at the kitchen table recalling a photograph of a handsome, smiling young man in Hazel's apartment. If Marty was the guy in the picture, it should be no problem to spend a couple of hours with him. He'd hopefully be pleasant and would be as much a gentleman as Hazel was strait-laced.

The next morning, Noelle met Silas at Althea's house and then walked him up the beach to the cottage. It was time to begin turning the seashells into Christmas ornaments. They'd done a few before, but now they had to work in earnest.

As they walked along the sand, Duke raced ahead of them and back again.

Silas looked up at her with a serious expression. "I think my Dad likes you, Noelle."

"Really? Why do you say that?"

"He told Dora you were a nice woman."

"Ah ... well, that settles it then. We are good friends." Noelle wanted to be very careful about letting Silas think there was more than that going on.

"King doesn't want you to go away," Silas said.

"And you?" Noelle asked, giving him a steady look.

He shrugged and kicked a sneakered foot at the sand. "Me either."

"I'm going to show you how we can still see each other and

talk to one another even if I'm back in Boston."

"Really?"

"Sure. Facetime and conference calls work very nicely. I'm not going to stop being your friend, Silas. I promise."

"Oh." His green eyes settled on her, and she couldn't resist hugging him.

Duke dropped a yellow tennis ball at her feet. She picked it up and threw it for him, wishing she could so easily make Silas happy.

At the cottage, they emptied the shells they'd most recently collected onto the kitchen table. As they'd done before, they picked out the ones most suitable to make into Christmas tree ornaments and then carefully washed and dried each one before coating them with mineral oil to make them shine.

Noelle said, "These look perfect, Silas. I'll glue the string on them. You figure out what messages you want to add, okay?"

Silas nodded and picked up the red pen Noelle had bought for the project.

"What should I say?" Silas asked.

"Anything you want. You could say Merry Christmas or send a message to Nana hoping she feels better, things like that. I'll print a few words out for you to use."

"Okay."

While Noelle glued the string to the shells, Silas silently wrote words.

"How do you spell sorry?" he asked, giving her a worried look.

"S-o-r-r-y," Noelle spelled out. "Why?"

Silas bit his lip and looked down at the piece of paper in front of him.

Noelle came over to him and wrapped an arm around him. "What is it, Silas?"

He turned into her, buried his face against her stomach,

and began to sob. "I ... I ... was bad. I talked back to ... Mom."

Noelle pulled a chair up next to his and took him in her arms. "Tell me what happened."

He lifted a tear-streaked face to her, misery clouding his eyes. "I talked back to Mom and then she died."

Noelle's pulse raced with alarm. "It's not your fault that your mother died, Silas. That was something nobody could start or stop from happening. It was something inside her that caused her to die."

Tears rolled down his cheeks. "But I never got to say I was sorry."

Noelle's mind raced to come up with healing things to say. "We'll put your note on a special shell and hang it on the tree. It's a beautiful way to say you're sorry, and somehow, I think she'll know it's there." Later, she'd tell Jake what she'd learned, and he and Dr. Heard could help Silas with this concern.

"I'll draw flowers on it too," said Silas, wiping his eyes with the back of his hand.

"Nice idea," said Noelle. She printed the word "sorry" on a piece of paper and handed it to him. "Here's how you spell sorry. Write whatever you wish you'd said to her. Okay?"

He nodded. "Okay."

As she continued to work on the shells, she watched Silas out of the corner of her eye. His tongue was caught between his lips as he concentrated on making the letters that meant so much to him.

When Silas was through with his note to his mother, he handed it to her. "There. It's done."

She looked down at it and blinked away the tears that stung her eyes. The words "I'm sorry, Mom" were surrounded by as many pink flowers as he could make.

"It's beautiful, Silas. Do you feel better now?"

He nodded. "I didn't mean to make her mad at me."

"Oh?"

"She sometimes got mad."

"Well, we all have moments when we're frustrated," Noelle said, wondering how much Silas knew of his parents' unhappiness. She had no intention of getting involved in something like that. "Did you make a note for Nana?"

"Not yet."

"Why don't you get to work on it? I'm almost finished gluing the string onto the shells."

A few minutes later, Silas handed Noelle a note: "I hope you feel better! Love Silas." Blue flowers were drawn around the letters.

"Very nice!" Noelle said, smiling at him. "How about another one?"

"I know. One for Dad."

They stopped for lunch and continued for another hour or so.

"Can we do something else now?" Silas said. "I've written a lot of notes."

"Yes. You've done a wonderful job. I'll glue them on tonight. Shall we go to the book store? I've thought of a book I need, and I'll get you a new book in one of your favorite series."

Silas's face lit up. "I want one about secrets."

"Okay, we'll ask for it." She loved that Silas liked to read.

Noelle dropped Silas off at home with a number of books. They'd spent time in the children's section of the book store discovering new books he wanted to read. She'd found a cookbook that had entire menus planned, along with ideas for table decorations, and easy three-step recipes.

Sitting in the kitchen at the cottage, Noelle sipped a cup of tea and glanced at the notes Silas had written. There was one each for his mother, Dad, Uncle Brett, Nana, Duke, Dora, his grandparents, and her. She'd seen all of the notes but hers. Silas had informed her that her message was to be a surprise. He'd carefully folded it up and sealed it with tape and then told her which seashell to use for it.

Eager to be able to clear the table before cooking dinner, Noelle sat down to finish up the work on the shells. She carefully wrapped a note around an olive shell and tied it in place with string. She glued another note to the back of a scallop shell. Where she didn't have enough purchase on a shell to tape or wrap a note, she folded it, wrapped the string around it like a package, and tied it to the string holding the shell. It was dark outside by the time all eight decorations were set. She carefully placed them with the other ornaments in a box, ready to take to Althea's house for the tree-trimming party planned later that week.

Noelle poured herself a glass of wine and picked up one of her new cookbooks. The sound of her cell rang into the quiet.

Noelle saw who it was and answered. "Hi, Jake! I'm so glad you called. Silas said something today that I thought you should know about." She told him about how guilty Silas felt about sassing his mother. "He said she used to get mad at him."

Jake let out a long sigh. "I'll talk to Silas about it and call Dr. Heard. Thanks. I really appreciate it. The reason I called was to see if you wanted to try cooking dinner on Friday."

"I'm so sorry, but I can't do it then. I have a date."

"Oh, I didn't realize ..."

"No, it's not what you think. Hazel Vogel's great-nephew was forced into calling me. He's the Plan B the ladies at the assisted-living community conjured up."

"What was Plan A?"

Noelle searched for an answer. "Something that didn't work out," she finally said. She wasn't about to tell him that Plan A included their desire for her to like the handsome, rich man with whom she'd been photographed in Miami. The very man who'd hired a private jet to get her to Boston.

"Those women really care for you, Noelle. That's nice."

She laughed. "I'll let you know how wonderful they are after my date on Friday. We'll see then how desperate they are for me to find someone. I've told them I'm not ready, but they won't believe me."

"Well, I'd better go. Maybe we can make our cooking dinner another night."

"Okay. Don't forget. Silas is planning a tree-trimming party surprise for Saturday night. You're going to receive a party invitation. Silas made you one this afternoon."

"I'll make sure I'm there," Jake said. "See you then."

Noelle clicked off the call and sat a moment thinking of Jake and his devotion to his son. Silas was lucky to have him for his father, and Jake was lucky to have a boy like Silas. She could no longer deny her feelings for Jake, but she'd do them both the favor and leave the idea of a relationship between Jake and her alone. He had trust issues and a little boy to protect if things did not go well.

CHAPTER SEVENTEEN

As Friday evening approached, Noelle wondered what she had been thinking to agree to go on a date with a man who'd been forced to ask her out. She'd been amused and he'd been so flustered that she'd never even discussed the best way to contact him. How foolish was that?

Noelle started to call Hazel to get more information about her great-nephew and then decided it would only cause a stir with the women. They'd want to know where they were going and what she was wearing. Then they'd ask her to give them all the details when the date was over.

She told her herself not to worry, if he didn't appear to be nice, she'd say she was sick and send him on his way.

On Friday, she left Althea's house without seeing Jake. He'd arrived home after accompanying his parents on a private flight to Tampa and then went back to the hospital to make sure everything was to their liking.

At the cottage, she took the time to soak in the tub. Submerged to her neck in warm water, Noelle lay back against the rim of the tub and let her thoughts drift. The days were getting much cooler with the approach of Christmas. Still, the weather in Boston was colder. She wondered what it would be like to live in Florida year-round and decided it might be a pleasant change. But then she thought of her family and of Edith, Hazel, Dorothy, and Rose and knew they were counting on her to be there for them.

Sighing, she got out of the tub and toweled herself off.

In her bedroom, Noelle studied the clothes in her closet

and decided to wear a pair of black slacks and a scoop-necked, long-sleeved knit top in white that was a perfect backdrop to showcase the bright-red, silk Gucci scarf she liked to wear at this time of year.

Noelle dressed and slid diamond studs into her earlobes and clasped a silver bracelet around her wrist. After putting on a touch of eye makeup, she fluffed her hair and considered herself ready for her date.

When she heard the slam of a car door outside the cottage, she checked her watch. Martin was on time. She swallowed nervously.

At the sound of the doorbell, she went to answer it, hoping this wasn't going to be one of those disappointing evenings she'd shake her head about for years.

Noelle opened the door and faced a young man who looked as worried as she. With blond hair cut short, handsome features that were nicely tanned, and a fit body, he gave her a tenuous smile.

"Noelle? I'm Martin."

Her lips curved. With his pink shirt, purple V-neck sweater and neatly pressed gray slacks, he was adorable. "Please come inside."

He stepped inside. "Thank you for agreeing to this date. It's very awkward, as you can see I'm ..."

"Gay," Noelle said, helping him to finish his sentence.

They grinned at each other and then broke out laughing.

"Hazel doesn't know?" Noelle said.

"I've tried to tell her, but you know how old-fashioned she is. She thinks it's just a phase I'm going through. Frankly, she isn't the only one in the family who thinks that way. Even so, I adore Aunt Hazel, and she's been very kind to me. I'm more than happy to do favors in return."

"And I'm that favor," Noelle said, unable to stop another

smile from spreading across her face.

"I've made dinner reservations at Gavin's, the restaurant at the Salty Key Inn not far from here. I hear the chef is great."

"How nice! I've wanted to go there," said Noelle. "But please, let's have an understanding that we will each pay for our own meal."

"Absolutely not," said Martin firmly. "A date is a date, and I'm going to do it the way Aunt Hazel would expect. And we're going to order anything we want. Agreed?"

Noelle nodded. "All right. Thank you very much. But I must warn you, I'm ready to try anything new."

He chuckled. "Me too. My partner, Chase Naughton, is a great cook, and he's teaching me how to cook a lot of different things."

"Perfect. You can tell me all about it, because I'm learning to cook too."

Gavin's was a fairly new restaurant that had gained a lot of notoriety for its pleasant setting and excellent food.

When they entered the restaurant, Noelle took a moment to look around. The wood-paneled dark walls were brightened by Oriental rugs, wall sconces, and candles flickering on the crowded tables.

They were seated at a table in a private nook that overlooked a small, tropical garden. Noelle let out a sigh of contentment. It was going to be a pleasant evening. On the way to the restaurant, she and Martin had chatted like old friends. And now, the delicious aromas wafting in the air made her mouth water in anticipation of a fabulous meal.

While they waited for the wine steward to take their order, Noelle took a moment to get a second look around. The dark, paneled walls were in contrast to the light, bright colors of the outdoors. The white-linen-covered tables held flickering candles in cut-glass votive holders and a hibiscus-shaped, white-porcelain container for a single, bright blossom. The main dining room was packed. At one side, a staircase led to the second floor, and she saw a number of people dressed for the holidays climb the stairs to one of the private rooms advertised as being upstairs.

"How about sharing a bottle of wine?" Martin asked. His hazel eyes twinkled. "Chase gave me some ideas for a bottle of red. I like pinot noir wines from Oregon. Do you have any other preferences?"

"A pinot sounds delightful," Noelle said. "I'm hungry for seafood, and that will go nicely."

The steward came to their table, and after discussing it with him, Martin placed an order for a pinot noir from the Willamette Valley, Oregon.

As Noelle perused the menu, she kept returning to an Alaskan salmon entrée that caught her eye.

Marvin announced he was going for the grilled chicken Mandarin style.

They placed their orders and sipped their wine, talking easily.

"Tell me about Hazel's family," she said to Martin. "I don't pry into any patient's personal lives but I'm willing to listen if they want to share. She has your photograph on her bureau, one of a young soldier in uniform, and a few of her little white dog. She must have siblings if she's an aunt."

"My mother and Hazel are the only two siblings. There's a big age difference between them. They grew up not knowing each other that well. As for being single, she was expecting to marry a young man who was killed early on in the Vietnam war. Nothing formal, just a promise."

"Thanks for telling me. Hazel is especially friendly with

three other women in the New Life Assisted-Living Community, and they've become fast friends. They call themselves The Three Musketeers Plus One. It's really nice to see."

Martin gave her a smile that warmed her heart. "That's where Plan B came in, I guess. Aunt Hazel made it very clear that I had no choice in the matter, that I was going to show you a wonderful evening. I wasn't sure what kind of person she had in mind for me, but she couldn't have chosen better. Too bad I'm already taken."

"That's what's made this so pleasant," said Noelle, beaming at him. "I hope I get to meet Chase sometime."

"He's a wonderful person. I'm lucky to have found him," said Martin, his eyes shining. "So, what are we going to tell Aunt Hazel?"

"I'm going to tell her I had a very pleasant evening, but like I've said all along, I'm not ready for a relationship with anyone just yet."

Martin thought a moment, then nodded. "That's fair. I'll have to handle my end differently, of course, but I do want her to know I did as she asked."

Noelle was surprised by how quickly the time had passed as they'd worked their way through the dessert course. She'd chosen a lemon souffle that was light and tasty.

After the bill had been paid, Martin helped her with her shawl and they walked out to his car.

On the way home, Noelle reviewed out loud one of the recipes Martin had told her about. "So, I make a honey and ginger marinade for the shrimp, and then after the shrimp is grilled, I ladle the sauce over the shrimp, which I place on a bed of brown rice."

"Yes, but don't forget the grilled pineapple. You can use that to garnish the plate, or simply place a few small slices on top of the shrimp. It looks like something hard to make, but it isn't."

"Thanks. I know exactly who I'm going to cook it for."

"Guy or gal?" Martin said.

"A man I've met here who loves to cook."

Martin quirked an eyebrow at her. "Are we talking about Plan A?"

Noelle laughed. "Close, but not exactly. We're just friends."

"Uh-huh," countered Martin. "You're blushing."

Noelle shook a playful finger at him. "Don't you dare mention this to Hazel. She and her friends think it's going to work, but it isn't. Jake and I have agreed that's how it is because there's so much more to the story."

"My lips are sealed. I promise," Martin said seriously, though a smile creased his face.

When they reached the cottage, Noelle turned to him. "Would you like to come in?"

"Thanks," said Martin, "but I need to get back to Sarasota. Chase and I are getting up early tomorrow to go fishing." He held up a finger. "Stay right there."

Martin got out of the car and hurried over to the passenger side to open the door for her.

She stepped out of the car onto the driveway and allowed him to walk her to the front door.

"Thanks again for a lovely evening," she said. Then, on tiptoes, she gave him a kiss on the cheek. "Keep in touch."

He smiled. "Let me know how it goes with Aunt Hazel."

"Will do." Noelle watched him walk away and then opened the door to the cottage. It had been a wonderful date—one she'd talk about happily.

The next morning Noelle awoke and stretched lazily. She'd

slept better than she had in some time. Her thoughts flew to the previous evening. Martin Vogel had turned out to be a delightful date. And today would be pleasant too. It was Silas's tree-trimming party.

She wrapped her robe around her and padded into the kitchen to fix herself a cup of coffee.

Above the sound of the coffee dripping into a pot, she heard the doorbell ring.

Puzzled, she went to answer it. Peering through the peephole in the door, she saw Jake. He was wearing jogging pants and a sweatshirt, and moving from one sneakered foot to the other.

She opened the door and waved him inside. "Cold morning, huh?"

He nodded. "Cold for Florida. Going to stay that way for a day or two."

"How about a hot cup of coffee?"

"Sounds great." Jake followed her into the kitchen and watched as she filled two cups.

She handed him a cup and indicated a place for him at the table. Lowering herself into a chair opposite him, she said, "What's up?"

"I thought I'd better talk to you about Silas. He's really excited about the tree-trimming party tonight. Dora is going to be there, along with Brett and his date, and I understand Gracie and her family are coming too."

"Yes, I'm proud of him for wanting to include her. They've been scouting for seashells together and have become new friends. We didn't think you'd mind."

"It's great. This is a way for Silas to connect to this area. I've been mulling things over, and I'm going to make some changes. I'm placing him in school here rather than having him return to his old school in New York. Dr. Heard and I agree it's a wise choice."

"So, you'd work from here?" Noelle couldn't hide her surprise. She took a sip of coffee and waited for him to answer.

"Here and South Beach. Brett will handle New York, and we'll both keep an eye on London. We have a very trustworthy partner in the London operation."

"Is Silas okay with this?" She imagined he'd be thrilled with it, but wanted to make sure.

"Yes. Apparently, he holds a lot of bad memories about New York. Florida is a healthy place for him. He loves the outdoors, and he and Duke can be much freer here."

"Will you live at Althea's?"

"No." He shook his head. "I'm buying a place a little farther down the beach. It's a house similar to hers, but with a pool so Silas can swim."

Noelle put a hand to her chest. "This is happening so quickly. But I can see by your smile how excited you are. I'm happy for you, Jake. I really am."

"Me, too." He took a sip of coffee and gazed out the kitchen window. "I've wanted to make a change, and I think this is the right one at the perfect time."

"More coffee? Cinnamon toast?"

Jake's eyes lit up. "Thanks. I'll have both. I can't remember the last time I had cinnamon toast. By the way, I was thinking that later this week we can do our first cooking lesson. I have to be here for an appointment with my parents."

"How are they doing?" Noelle asked, rising to put a couple of slices of bread into the toaster oven. "Are they happy with the rehab center?" She poured more coffee into his cup.

Jake made a face. "Dad isn't an easy patient. He's fighting to leave the rehabilitation center and come to Nana's house where extra private nursing can be made available, if necessary. In fact, both he and my mother are planning to make it to Silas's party."

Noelle caught her lip. Jake and Brett had accepted her bossiness, but what would his parents think of how she'd disrupted things?

Jake caught hold of her free hand and gave it a squeeze. "Don't worry. They already know how you've helped Silas and every one of us."

She nodded but couldn't help the thread of worry weaving through her. The toaster oven buzzed and she turned away to fix their toast. She'd have no choice but to be herself. Besides, she'd be leaving soon, and what they thought of her shouldn't be more important than taking care of Silas.

Noelle's cell sounded. She knew who it was and let it keep chiming.

Jake frowned at her. "Need to get that?"

"No. I'll call her back."

Her cell stopped chiming, and then started up again.

"You'd better get that," Jake said.

Sighing, she lifted the phone to her ear. "Hello, Hazel. How are you?"

"Good," said Hazel. "Edith, Rose and Dorothy are here with me. I'm putting you on speaker phone. We want to know how your date with Martin went."

"My date with Martin was wonderful. He's a great guy and we had a lot of fun. He's learning to cook like me, and we have some great recipes to share."

"And?" said Edith.

"And he's happy with his life right now and isn't interested in doing anything different. We've agreed to be friends, but that's as far as it's going."

"Oh, I see," said Rose.

"Back to Plan A," someone whispered in the background.

"Don't worry about Plan A," Noelle said. "I'm here for just

a few more weeks. I'll see you in the middle of next month."

"But he's perfect for you," said Edith.

"I know he's perfect, but it's not going anywhere. Trust me."

Noelle's cheeks flamed with heat when she realized Jake was listening closely to every word at her end of the conversation.

"Look, I'd better go," she said. "I have company."

"Is it Plan A?" Dorothy asked.

"Goodbye," Noelle said, and clicked off the call before she got into further trouble.

Jake's soft-gray gaze rested on her. "I take it your date went well last night."

"Yes. Martin is a great guy, everything I'd want in a man with just one problem."

Jake shot her a worried look. "Is he married?"

"No, he's about to be engaged to his lover, Chase, who, I'm told, is another great guy."

"He's gay?"

Noelle nodded. "Hazel doesn't realize it's more than a phase. Martin's family situation is not that great. He's more or less stepped away from them, except for his Aunt Hazel."

"So, then what is this Plan A?" Jake's eyes filled with amusement.

"That, my friend, is something I'm not even going to get into with you." To avoid any further questions, she said. "How about making a shrimp dish for our first cooking session? Martin gave me a wonderful recipe idea."

Jake chuckled softly. "It sounds perfect. Give me a list of the ingredients to bring and we'll cook together. Right now, I'd better get back to a very excited little boy. He's going to help Dora bake some cookies. I'll take care of the rest of the food."

"Should I bring something to the party?"

He shook his head. "Just your unique self." The look he gave her was more than friendly. It was as sexy as she'd seen.

Noelle's breath caught as he leaned toward her and then, at the last minute, he pulled away.

"See you tonight. Six o'clock." He gave her a little salute and headed for the front door.

She followed behind, showed him out, and leaned back against the door wondering if he was actually about to kiss her.

Noelle straightened and told herself she'd imagined it. But thinking of that moment, desire swept through her.

CHAPTER EIGHTEEN

Noelle looked in the mirror wondering what Jake's parents would see. Both Brett and Jake knew she was not interested in their money, their name, or the privileges that came from owning hotels. She was attractive but not glamorous, eager to learn new things but not worldly.

She imagined Jake's parents were all of those things.

For the party she'd chosen to wear her winter-white slacks, a black sweater and the red Gucci scarf she'd worn the night before. The red in the scarf always made her feel festive.

She decided to take a box of special, imported chocolates to the party. She'd recently discovered them in Boston and had found the same brand at the local gourmet store.

Armed with the candy, two boxes of the shell ornaments, and her determination to relax and let the evening unfold, she got into her car and drove to Althea's.

As she walked into Althea's kitchen, Silas ran over to her. "Do you have the shells?" He clapped a hand over his mouth. "I mean the decorations, Noelle?"

"Yes, they're here just like we packed them. Do you want to carry the one with the notes to the tree in the living room?"

He held out his arms, and Noelle placed the smaller box in them. The shells represented so much more than Christmas decorations. The hours spent together building a strong friendship were precious to each of them.

Dora came over to her. "Guess you missed all the excitement. Willis and Stephanie Bellingham moved in this morning. We have two new nurses, and I've become the temporary housekeeper."

"I'm glad Jake's parents were well enough to leave the rehabilitation center. But how do you feel about your new position?"

Dora's smile brightened her face. "I'm delighted! It's just temporary because Jake has already spoken to me about being the housekeeper at his new home."

"Oh, how wonderful! I bet Silas is happy about that."

"Can't say anything about it yet. The sale of the house doesn't go through for another week or so. It's going to be a Christmas surprise for Silas."

"Okay. Glad to know that," said Noelle, impressed by how fast things were happening. When Jake made up his mind about something, he moved quickly. "Where are Jake's parents now?"

"In the living room," said Dora. "This sure is a nice party for Silas. He has you to thank for most of it." Dora gave her a quick hug. "Now, go say hello to everyone."

Carrying the large box of shells, Noelle walked into the living room. All eyes turned to her. She fought the urge to run, and, instead, smiled. "Happy Tree Trimming, everyone!"

"To those who haven't already met her, this is Noelle North," Jake announced, smiling at her.

Silas ran over to her and took her hand. "Noelle is my friend. Decorating the tree is our secret," he said to the others proudly. Noelle smiled at him and glanced at the people in the room. Brett was standing next to a tall blonde who was clinging to his arm possessively. Next to her parents, Gracie waved at her. Seated next to Jake on the couch were two people who had to be Willis and Stephanie Bellingham. Her gaze swung back to Jake before facing the whole group.

Noelle placed the box she was carrying on the carpet by the tree and straightened. "Silas and I decided to do this together to make his Christmas tree very special this year, something he could always remember."

"It's seashells!" cried Silas, jumping up and down in his excitement. He ran over to the smaller box and lifted the lid. Inside, the shells were piled in a mixture of shapes with various markings.

"What a lovely idea," Stephanie said.

"And I have secret messages for you!" Silas picked up one of the labeled shells and handed it to his grandmother. "It's a moon shell."

"Shall I read the message now?" she asked Silas.

He shook his head. "Not until Christmas. It's my secret present."

"Okay, then, I'll keep it in a special place until then," she replied, her eyes glistening with tears. "This is going to be the best Christmas ever—a holiday I thought I'd never see."

Silas quickly handed out his notes to everyone else and then turned to her. "I don't have one for Gracie," he whispered loudly.

"Why don't you give her the pretty red scallop shell? That looks most like Christmas."

Silas turned to Gracie. "I have a special Christmas shell for you. It's the one you wanted when I found it. Remember?"

Gracie beamed and nodded her head. "Thankth, Thilath."

Looking on as Silas handed the shell to Gracie, Noelle felt a surge of love for the little boy who'd won her affection from the beginning. She wouldn't be standing here now if it weren't for Silas.

"Before we get started on decorating the tree," Jake announced, "we've put out some refreshments in the dining room. Please help yourselves to whatever you wish to drink, the cookies Silas and Dora made, and all the other offerings."

As people headed for the dining room, Jake held Noelle

back. "I want you to meet my parents."

Jake led her over to his parents and made the introductions.

"Nice to meet you, Noelle," said his father. "I've heard a lot of good things about you."

"Yes," added Jake's mother. "Come sit down by me. I'd like to know more."

"I'll bring you a glass of wine," Jake said to Noelle, grinning at his mother. "You might need it."

"On your way, son." Smiling, Stephanie playfully motioned for Jake to leave. A pretty woman with blond hair whose gray roots were still showing from her time in the woods, she had the same gray eyes as her son. They shone with curiosity as her gaze swept over Noelle.

Bracing herself for a lot of questions, Noelle sat down in a chair next to Stephanie. "I'm so happy you and your husband were found alive."

"Thank you. I appreciate that. Now, young lady, tell me about yourself."

Winking at Noelle, Willis said to his wife, "Now go easy on her, Steph."

Noelle swallowed hard.

Stephanie turned to her. "Brett calls you the bossy nurse, and Jake tells me you and Silas are very close. How did this all come about?"

Fighting the dryness in her throat, Noelle explained the impact Silas had had on her from the beginning, how angry she'd been to see Althea abused, and how she'd automatically reacted to it.

"Of course, Jake was a little upset with me for barging into his family like that," said Noelle. "But he soon understood."

Stephanie grinned. "You boss my sons around and get them to accept what you say? I adore you! We've needed someone like you around." She lowered her voice. "Not like that silly girl Brett brought to the party. She's hanging onto him as if he's going to disappear like a ghost of a Christmas past, taking all her gifts away."

Surprised by Stephanie's confiding in her, Noelle didn't know what to say. She was relieved when Jake approached with a glass of wine for her.

"Can I get you and Dad anything?" Jake asked his mother.

Stephanie turned to her husband. "We probably shouldn't have any alcohol with the medications we're taking."

"Who says? A small glass of wine isn't going to hurt," Willis said. "Make mine scotch."

Noelle couldn't help smiling. For a moment, Willis had looked exactly like Jake when he was teasing her.

Once everyone had enjoyed refreshments, Dora wheeled Althea into the room to watch as the tree trimming began. Hearing people exclaim over the shells and observing the green boughs of the tree take on a different look, Noelle filled with pride at all she and Silas had accomplished. She estimated at least fifty shells were hanging on the branches.

'What about a Chrithmath thtar?" said Gracie.

Silas turned to Noelle. "We have to wait for the perfect one. Right?"

Noelle nodded. "We're still looking for it. We've got a little time left to find it."

"Can I look for one too?" said Gracie.

Noelle looked to Silas.

"Okay," said Silas. "But if you find one, it's mine."

"We'll have to see about that," said Noelle pleasantly.

When Gracie's parents indicated it was time for them to leave, Noelle decided she'd leave too. She went to the kitchen to get her things.

"Where are you going?" Jake asked, joining her.

"I thought I'd give your family time to be together. After all you and your parents have been through, it seems only right."

"What's right is for you to stay. My mother likes you a lot." He smiled at her. "I do too."

Noelle hesitated.

"Please," Jake said quietly. "I'd like it if you would stay for a while longer."

At the quiet pleading in his voice, Noelle agreed to postpone leaving. She was as curious about his family as they seemed to be about her.

Conversation continued pleasantly, but it soon became clear that Willis and Stephanie were exhausted. As Dora prepared to escort them upstairs, Stephanie waved Noelle to her side. "It was nice meeting you. I know I'll be seeing more of you. Silas adores you, and I see how Jake looks at you."

Noelle could feel her cheeks grow warm and wished she could hide her feelings.

"Neither of you may realize it yet, but you're a perfect match. I probably shouldn't say something like this when I barely know you, but a mother understands such things about her children."

Jake came over to them. Frowning, he said to his mother, "What are you talking about?"

She waved away his concern. "Just girl talk. That's all." She winked at Noelle. "Good night, Noelle. See you soon."

Noelle stood beside Jake and watched Stephanie leave the room on Dora's arm.

"She seems like such a warm, wonderful woman," said Noelle.

"Beware. Beneath all that charm lies a woman as strong as steel. She's been a great match for my father."

Noelle thought of Stephanie's words to her. Were she and Jake a perfect match?

Brett came over to them. "Cherie and I are heading up to Clearwater to see what's happening. We'll spend the night there. With Mom and Dad here, there's not enough room for us."

"Okay," Jake said. "Makes sense."

Brett leaned over and gave Noelle a kiss on the cheek. "Great job with the tree decorations. Silas is thrilled with it."

"Thanks. We both have learned a lot about shells, and I think it turned out well."

"It sure has made a different holiday for all of us," Brett said. He punched Jake's arm playfully. "Later, bro."

Noelle and Jake were left alone in the room. "Care for another glass of wine? You hardly touched yours earlier."

She grinned. "Sounds lovely. I was sitting with your mother, and she kept me talking."

After Jake left the room, Noelle took a seat on the living room couch where she could study the tree. She'd come to Florida because she hadn't wanted to celebrate Christmas. Now, she was glad Silas had forced her to do so. It wasn't like Christmases of the past. This was something very new. And, she admitted to herself, her happiness had a lot to do with Jake. He'd changed. If, like she thought, he was interested in something more than friendship, she was ready to see where it would lead.

The small, white lights on the Christmas tree twinkled at her and shone light on the shells that hung from the branches, Christmas treasures from the sea. The decorations had cost nothing more than time and effort on Silas's part and hers, yet it was the most beautiful tree she'd ever seen. She stared at the shell with her message taped to it and wondered what it said. Hers to Silas would have said, "Thank you for the best

Christmas ever."

Jake returned to the living room with two glasses of wine and sat down beside her. "This evening has been great for so many reasons. The look of joy on Silas's face when the tree was decorated is something I won't forget for a long time. And to think my parents were here to see it!" He shook his head. "I can't believe all that's happened so fast."

"Yes, and now you're getting a new house and setting up a work schedule you can live with. I'm truly happy for you."

He set down his glass on the coffee table, took hers from her hand, and placed it beside his. Gazing steadily into her eyes, he leaned toward her. "I've wanted to do this for a long time." His lips came down on hers, gentle and soft.

Noelle closed her eyes and took in all the sensations running through her body in electrifying jolts.

His kiss deepened, and he tugged her toward him.

Noelle went into his arms, loving the feel of them wrapped around her, making her feel treasured in a way she hadn't felt before.

Silas ran into the room and stopped in front of them. "Hey! What are you doing?"

Noelle jerked away from Jake, dizzy from the jarring sound of Silas's voice.

"Noelle and I were testing to see if the mistletoe Gracie's parents brought here works." Jake smiled. "It really does."

Silas studied them both. "Okay. I get to watch television upstairs. Gran said I could watch with her." He gave them a quick wave and ran out of the room.

"That wasn't as hard to explain as I thought it might be," said Jake. "It's what Silas has wanted all along."

"We have to be careful, Jake. This is the very beginning of what might or might not work for us, and I don't want to see Silas hurt."

"I don't want any of us hurt," Jake said quietly. "But I'm willing to trust you and what I'm feeling. That feeling isn't new, you know. When I first saw you in your bathrobe that first morning, I thought you were adorable. And when you made it clear you weren't going to be intimidated by the situation or me, I fell for you then. It wasn't until after talking to Dr. Heard that I felt I could deal with trusting that feeling and you. I do love you, you know."

Noelle sat facing him, clutching her hands. "The only thing I ask is that if you change your mind about us, you let me know right away."

"How do *you* feel about us?" Jake asked, clasping her cold fingertips in his.

Noelle took a deep breath and stared into his eyes. "I'm willing to see where it leads. That's saying a lot. I've stayed away from relationships for almost two years."

"We've both been wounded, Noelle. I'm not going to hurt you. I promise."

He kissed her so tenderly, she kept her eyes closed, afraid he might see her tears. His parents being alive was a miracle. Were his mother's words about Jake and her being perfect for each other part of the miracle too?

CHAPTER NINETEEN

The next morning, Noelle awoke with a new sense of wonder. Had she just dreamed about kissing Jake? When she realized it was true, she felt her lips curve. She lifted a hand to them, remembering the taste of him, how he'd held her, the way he'd made her insides curl with pleasure. She'd once thought she knew what it was like to feel love for a man, but this was different. Even though it was just the beginning of what they each hoped would be a lasting, loving, trustworthy relationship, her feelings for Jake were deeper and more multi-dimensional than she'd ever experienced.

Noelle liked that Jake hadn't pushed for more than she was ready to give, though she was already thinking about what it would be like to make love with him.

She got up, took a quick shower, and dressed for the day fueled with a fresh energy that came from optimism. Was it possible that within weeks she'd fallen in love?

In the kitchen, while a pot of fresh coffee was brewing, she fixed a bowl of oatmeal. As she finished eating it, her cell phone chimed.

Smiling, she picked up the call. "Hi, Mom! How are you?"

"My! You sound cheerful this morning. I'm fine. How are things down there?"

"Good. I've met some new people, and the little boy I'm helping had a tree-trimming party that was very nice."

"Oh, nice! It sounds as if you're making friends."

Noelle chose the safest subjects she could. No way would she tell her mother about her evening with Jake. "Gracie is a little girl who sometimes accompanies Silas and me on shelling walks. Her parents are lovely. I particularly like her mother. In fact, we've promised to remain in touch even after I leave here."

"I love when women make connections like that," said her mother.

"Have you finished all the decorations for the house?" Noelle asked, changing the subject. Her mother usually did an outstanding job of decorating their home. Thinking of it now, Noelle felt a touch of homesickness and quickly dismissed it.

"This year I've outdone myself, if I say so," said her mother. "Most of the neighbors on our street have decorated outside so it seems like a winter wonderland when you drive into our area. Have you done any decorating to that little cottage?"

Noelle surprised herself by saying, "Not yet."

"It's late enough in the season that you might be able to pick up some things on sale." Her mother sighed. "I still wish you hadn't made the decision to leave Boston for the holidays. I know how hurt you've been, but, darling, you can't let that awful man ruin your life."

"I know, Mom. I'm working on it."

A knock sounded at the door.

"Look! I've got to go. I'll talk to you later. Love you!"

Noelle hung up the phone certain now that she'd done the right thing by coming to Florida for the holidays. And when she opened the door to find Jake standing there smiling at her, that thought was easily reconfirmed.

He held out a small paper bag. "Dora sent you some cookies and treats from last night."

"Want to come in?"

He grinned. "You bet."

As he stepped inside, the entire interior of the cottage seemed to brighten.

He paused a moment, gazing into her eyes.

She stood still, feeling herself drawn into them and reading the message there.

Jake set the bag on a table, and they moved toward each other.

"It wasn't a dream," Noelle whispered, and met his lips with hers.

When they finally drew apart, Jake clasped her face in his strong hands and smiled. "I had to be sure. I love you, Noelle."

"I love you too," she said, feeling that emotion deep within her.

He kissed her again, and then picked up the bag of cookies. "Let's celebrate! I smell coffee."

She laughed. "I've just made a fresh pot. Come into the kitchen. I'll pour you a cup."

As Noelle poured the coffee for Jake, she wondered what living with him would be like. At Althea's she'd seen how accommodating he was to everyone else. And Dora was thrilled to be asked to be his housekeeper. That was an important sign.

She sat opposite him at the kitchen table. "What do you have planned for today?"

"I'm going to do a walk-through of the house I'm buying. Won't you come with me? I'd like a woman's perspective on what might need to be done."

"Sure. I love looking at houses." She was careful not to read too much into his invitation. Deciding to see where a relationship was going didn't mean moving in right away or getting married. They'd both promised to take their time.

Jake set down his coffee cup. "I have something to tell you."

"Okay," she replied, wondering why his lips had formed a smile.

"Silas and I were alone in the kitchen this morning when

he said, 'I saw you kissing Noelle. Does that mean she's making a baby?'"

Noelle couldn't hold back a laugh. "Oh my God! What did you say?"

Jake chuckled. "I told him that kissing someone doesn't mean they'll make a baby. And he said, and I quote, 'Good! Because Gracie gave me a kiss the other day.'"

Noelle and Jake laughed together. Then he grew serious.

"Silas then asked, 'Are you going to marry Noelle?'"

Noelle looked at him. "And you said?"

"I said I wanted to marry you, but it might be a while before that happens. Silas told me that's what he wants for Christmas. I thought I'd better give you a heads-up. He might say something like that to you."

Noelle let out a sigh. "The last thing I want to do is to hurt Silas, but these things usually take time."

"I don't want to rush you," said Jake. "But I love you and once I make up my mind about something I tend to move fast."

Noelle smiled. "I know. The house."

"It's a very nice house that's perfect for a family. I wanted a lot of children, but Claire said no more after having Silas, something about it ruining her figure."

The sadness in Jake's voice touched Noelle. "I've always wanted a lot of kids too. And when I see my parents with my brothers' children, I realize how special it would be for them."

"You mean you want children of your own?" Jake's gaze bored into her, and she realized how important the question was for him.

"Oh, yes. But do you think it's late for me to start having a lot of children?"

"Nonsense," said Jake. "Look at you! You're in great shape." His sexy smile sent a shiver of desire through her.

"Come here."

She went to him and settled on the lap he offered her. Nestled against his sturdy chest, she could hear the racing of his heart. He held her close and stroked her back with the palm of his hand.

"You'd make a wonderful mother, Noelle. I've seen how you are with Silas, and even with Gracie." He lifted her chin and lowered his lips to hers.

When they pulled apart, his smile lit his eyes. "I wish I could show you how I really feel, but that will have to wait. My phone is alerting me that it's time to meet the real estate salesperson at the house. Will you come with me?"

Shaken out of the daze from his kiss, Noelle now heard the pinging of his phone. She got to her feet and stood back as Jake rose.

He swept her in his arms and gave her a kiss that indicated how much he wanted to stay.

Once more, his phone pinged.

Muttering softly, Jake moved away from her and grabbed his phone. Grinning wickedly, he said, "Later, we can pick up right where we left off."

Noelle smiled and remained silent, too emotional to respond. She'd never been kissed like that before. Her entire body felt as if it was melting. She grabbed hold of the edge of the table.

"You okay?" Jake asked.

Trying to slow her beating heart, Noelle nodded. "Give me a moment, and I'll be ready to go."

Inside her bedroom, Noelle walked over to the mirror. The person who gazed back at her with eyes full of wonder looked like an entirely new Noelle North. One she hadn't seen before. It was an image she liked a lot.

###

Penny Patterson, an older woman with blond hair styled in a bob, met them in the driveway of a large, white-stucco house. She gazed with interest at Noelle as she shook hands with Jake.

"And who is this?" Penny asked politely.

"Noelle North, a special friend of mine," Jake answered. "She's agreed to take a look at the house with me and make notes of any changes I might like."

"Welcome, both of you. As you will see, Noelle, Jake has made a fine choice of a house for him and his son. It's a lovely property, and Jake was wise to move so quickly to buy it. A number of disappointed people have agreed to be on a waiting list for it, should he change his mind."

"I'm eager to see it," Noelle said, taking note of how quickly he was making the purchase happen.

The exterior of the sprawling, one-story house was attractive, clean, and well maintained. A gray tile roof capped the structure, and the landscaping around it was lovely.

Noelle stood in the living room looking out at the screened lanai, charmed by the sight of the turquoise water of the splash pool and spa outside offset by colorful flowers and palms in planters strategically placed to give privacy to the space. As they walked through the house, Noelle discovered the lanai served as the center of the house and was easily accessed through sliding doors from the living room, the master suite in one wing of the house, and one bedroom and the family room in the other wing. The house had five bedrooms and four and a half baths, making it perfect for family and guests.

"What do you think?" asked Jake, standing in the middle of the large, modern kitchen and gazing around.

"It's a beautiful house," Noelle said. "I can see why people are willing to be placed on a waiting list."

"Yes, but what work does it need before I move in?"

"Okay. You asked. Here's what I'd do. I'd have the tile floors throughout cleaned and resealed, the bedroom suite at the far end repainted and carpeted for Dora, and the carpeting replaced in the master suite. Other than that, it looks great. Someone has taken care of this place."

Jake studied their surroundings and nodded. "They might not have had a black lab and a seven-year-old boy to mess things up."

"It's a great house for Silas and Duke. You have enough room for Dora and to add to your family."

Penny walked into the kitchen. "What do you think, Noelle? And, Jake, every item on the home inspection list has been done to our satisfaction. Right?"

"Yes, I've gone over it and checked things out on my own," Jake said, "but Noelle has some suggestions, and I'm wondering if you can give me the name of a reliable company to refinish the tile flooring."

"Not a problem. I've got a great guy in mind. It's on a list I've made with all the service people you might need." Penny turned to Noelle. "It's a lovely home, isn't it?"

"Oh, yes." Noelle indicated the space with a wide sweep of her arm. "Any family would be lucky to live here."

"You're a special friend?" Penny asked, studying her.

Jake wrapped his arm around Noelle's shoulder. "More than a friend, I hope."

"I thought so," said Penny. "Noelle, do you have a house that will need to be sold?"

Amused by her aggressiveness, Noelle said, "I'm just a visitor here, but thank you."

Penny checked her watch. "I have another appointment. But, if you like, you may stay to take measurements or to make more notes. Just leave the key in the lockbox. You have the code for it."

After she left, Jake turned to Noelle. "Can you see yourself living here? With Silas and me?"

She knew he was asking much more than that and smiled at him. "Yes."

He drew her into his arms. "I can't wait for that to happen. I know you want to go slowly, and I'll try to do that for you." But when he kissed her, she knew right away how hard it would be for him to do that.

When they pulled apart, he took her hand. "Let's sit by the pool for a while and talk. I want to know everything about you. And though you probably know a lot more about me, you can ask me anything."

"Anything?" she teased.

"Yup. If we're going to make this work, we need to know the good, the bad, and the ugly about one another."

Noelle shot him a playful smile. "Can I start with the good?"

He laughed. "I don't know. We might never get to the bad."

With the sound of the waterfall from the spa into the pool in the background, Noelle and Jake started their conversation. A while later, Noelle went to get them a glass of water with the paper cups the real estate agent had left on the counter, and they continued talking.

Two hours later, Noelle realized she knew more about Jake than she'd ever really known about Alex. She liked that Jake was so open and wondered if his visits with Dr. Heard had helped him become this way. She, in turn, was able to be honest about herself and found that he was a sympathetic listener.

By the time they left the house that might one day be hers, Noelle was comfortable with her growing relationship with Jake. When he'd asked her to stay in Florida to give their relationship a chance to survive, her answer was easy to give. After making a foolish mistake, she wanted to go forward. He was the kind of man she'd been waiting for all her life.

CHAPTER TWENTY

When Jake and Noelle walked into Althea's house, Jake's mother was sitting at the kitchen table eating lunch.

"There you are," Stephanie said. "I've been hoping to see you. What's all this talk about kissing and making babies and a Christmas star that Silas is talking about?"

Noelle and Jake glanced at one another and exchanged smiles.

"Silas saw me kissing Noelle last night."

Stephanie waved them both to chairs at the kitchen table. "Sit. Both of you. And tell me exactly what's going on."

Noelle and Jake each responded to the command in her voice.

She studied them both. "Is it true? There's really something happening between the two of you? If so, I couldn't be more delighted. But if there's a baby on the way, we'd better talk about a wedding sooner rather than later."

Jake chuckled. "Wait until you hear the story behind Silas's remark." By the time Jake finished, all three of them were laughing.

"Even though there's no baby, don't wait too long, Jake," said Stephanie. "Noelle is a treasure. Brett adores her too."

"You've been talking about us?" Jake said, arching his eyebrow at his mother.

"Absolutely. I saw how you were with her last night and needed to find out more. Your brother wasn't happy that I called and woke him up this morning, but he was very cooperative." She reached over and patted Noelle's hand. "You see what it's like trying to get information from men?"

Noelle nodded. "Oh, yes, I know all about it. I have three older brothers."

"That's why she's so bossy," Jake said grinning at Noelle.

"She, my son, is what is needed in this family as I get older."

"I couldn't agree more," Jake replied, serious now.

Stephanie rose to her feet with a little grunt of pain and bent down to give Noelle a kiss on her cheek. "I hope everything works out between the two of you. I'd love to welcome you as my daughter. In the meantime, I promised my grandson I'd watch a movie with him this afternoon."

Jake got up from his chair and walked his mother out of the room.

Minutes later Silas burst into the kitchen. "Hi, Noelle. My dad says he wants to marry you."

"Silas," she said calmly. "That's what we hope, but we have to wait and see."

"I know," Silas said. "I made a secret wish, and if we find the perfect Christmas star, I know it'll come true."

Silas ran out of the room before Noelle could say anything more.

Dora walked into the kitchen carrying a tray from Althea's room.

"How is she today?" Noelle asked.

"Not doing as well as other days. I got her to eat a little food, but I'm concerned. She has no appetite. She's on the porch in her wheelchair if you want to speak to her."

Noelle got to her feet. "Thanks, I'll go check on her."

Outside, Noelle pulled up a chair next to Althea's wheelchair and took hold of her hand. "How are you today, Althea? It's a nice, bright day."

Wrapped in a warm blanket, Althea squinted her eyes. "You're not Claire."

"No," said Noelle. "I'm not. I'm Noelle. I came here to help you."

Althea's eyes brightened and a moment of recognition filled them. "Yes. You saved me." The light in her eyes faded. "Nice day." Humming, she stared out at the beach and the water beyond.

Noelle continued to hold her hand. It seemed like months had passed not just weeks since she'd first encountered the Bellingham family. Now she might end up being part of it.

Jake stepped onto the porch and smiled at her. "Dora said you might be here."

"The water is soothing to her. I'm glad she has this spot where she can relax."

"Mom and Dad are going to move in here for a while, instead of moving back to either of their places in New York or Miami."

"That will be easier for them."

"Yes, they want to be able to keep Nana here as long as possible, and it will be great for Silas to have them close by."

He held out his hand. "Care to take a walk?"

"Sure. Want to head up to the cottage? I forgot my phone."

They called to Dora to tell her they were leaving, and then went out to the beach. Though the air was cool, the sun was warm on Noelle's face as she lifted it to the sun. Her mind spun with the idea of living with Jake and Silas in a house along the Gulf Coast of Florida.

Waves rolled in and kissed the shore, their frothy edges lining the beach in a pretty pattern. A trio of pelicans skimmed the surface of the water, like pilots flying in formation in an air show. The cries of seagulls swirled in the air like the birds themselves. It would be a totally different lifestyle for her here, but one she couldn't wait to try.

Out of the corner of her eye, she watched Jake move with

fluid, long strides. He was a man who could easily oversee big business operations and handle being in charge of hundreds of people. But, now, she knew how little that mattered compared to the family he had and the one he hoped to create with her.

It seemed incredible that they could fall in love so quickly and deeply in such a short time. But she, like Jake, knew their growing relationship was something precious to each of them and they'd vowed not to hurt each other. That meant a lot to her. Without that commitment to trust, she might continue to hold back. Now, she couldn't wait to let him know her real feelings toward him.

At the cottage, she found her phone where she'd left it in the kitchen. Checking for messages, she smiled. Hazel Vogel had called. No doubt she and her three friends had gathered around her phone to check on her.

"Anything important?" Jake said.

"The ladies at New Life are checking up on me again," she responded, smiling.

"Where is New Life? Someplace west of Boston, right?"

"Yes. Not far from Newton, where my parents live."

Jake came up behind her and nuzzled her neck. "Maybe the day will come when you have a lot for those women to talk about. Huh?"

She turned around and went into his arms. "Maybe some things I won't talk about."

He laughed. "You make me happy, Noelle."

She let out a sigh of satisfaction and snuggled up against him.

###

When Noelle and Jake returned to Althea's house, Silas was in the living room playing with his collection of dragons, and Stephanie and Willis were taking late afternoon naps. Silas jumped to his feet when he saw them and ran over to Noelle.

"Can we look for our Christmas star?"

"It's getting dark, but we have a little time to look. C'mon. I'll walk you down to the beach."

"I'll be right back." Silas went to grab his jacket.

"The idea of the perfect Christmas star is taking on more meaning than I think is healthy," said Noelle. "But after all the work we've done on the rest of the tree, I think it's important to follow through."

"I agree," said Jake. "I'm going to cook dinner for the family. Want to help?"

"Later. Dora is due her night off, and the night nurse won't be here for another two hours. Silas and I won't be gone long."

"Okay. I'll check in with Dora."

On the beach, Silas took Noelle's hand and looked up at her. "What does a Christmas star look like?"

"We can use anything we want for our Christmas star. When we find something unique, you can decide if that's what you want."

"I'm going to look for the perfect thing," announced Silas. "And when we put it on top of the tree, you'll find my secret message. Poppy helped me put your shell right near the top. You can't read my message until we find our star."

"Okay, I promise I won't touch it."

Silas moved ahead, walking slowly, his face to the ground.

When it grew too dark to continue looking, they went back to the house. Stephanie and Willis were sitting together on the living room couch, enjoying a cocktail.

"Come join us," said Stephanie. "Willis hasn't had much of a chance to talk to you, and it's important."

"All right, I will. First, I'll check on Althea and Jake to make sure I'm not needed there."

"Of course, dear," said Stephanie. She nudged her husband. "See what I mean? She's her own person. I love that."

Willis studied Noelle and nodded.

Noelle hurried into the kitchen with Silas.

"Any luck?" Jake asked Silas.

Silas shook his head. "Not yet."

"We'll look tomorrow morning," said Noelle. They were running out of time. Christmas was just four days away.

While Silas stayed in the kitchen with his father, Noelle returned to the living room. As much as she dreaded what she considered to be an interview, she needed to know how Willis felt about her being with his son. Jake had mentioned that Willis was fond of Claire, and she and Claire were nothing alike.

Noelle sat in a chair next to the couch. "How are both of you feeling? I can't imagine what you've gone through."

"Each day is better than the last," said Willis. "I'm just grateful to be alive."

"As everyone is," agreed Stephanie, giving her husband a pat on the shoulder. "He's my hero."

Noelle smiled. "Jake said the same thing about both of you."

"You're from Boston, I'm told," said Willis. "What has brought you to Florida for the holidays?"

"A restlessness for something different, I suppose you could say. I'm the health care supervisor for the New Life Assisted-Living Community, and four of my favorite women there ganged up on me and told me I needed a change. They're the ones who found Seashell Cottage for rent."

"I heard all about how you protected my mother from a caretaker who never should have been allowed to attend her." Willis' direct gaze made Noelle shift in her chair. "I want to personally thank you for that. Normally, I'd do something nice in return, something monetary in fact. But I've been warned not to offer it to you. Is that correct?"

"Yes," said Noelle firmly. "I wouldn't take it anyway."

"Stephanie has been filling me in on your family. Three older brothers." He chuckled. "That would make any girl strong."

"Oh, yes. I learned how to deal with them early on. But I love them. We're a close family. My mother has always been active in the community, and my father was a professor at Boston College and is now retired. That's how I was able to attend nursing school there."

"How old are you?" Willis asked, leaning forward, waiting for her answer.

Before she could answer, Stephanie said, "Don't answer that, Noelle." She turned to her husband. "Willis, men don't ask women about their age. I thought I taught you better."

Willis gave Noelle an apologetic look. "Guess I've been corrected on that score. But I must say, I admire your spunk and willingness to step in and help others. I understand you've even helped Jake with an assessment of his new house. I like that." He smiled at Stephanie and turned back to Noelle. "Steph and I have been married for forty-five years. We were just young kids when we married, but we've made it work by being a team, working together and raising our children together. Sounds like our families are similar. I like that."

Jake came into the living room carrying a glass of wine. "I thought you might like this, Noelle." He handed her the glass of wine and turned to his parents. "How'd the job interview go?"

Willis had the grace to give him a sheepish look. "Sorry, son. I've never seen you so happy and wanted to find out more about the woman who's making you feel that way."

Jake put an arm around Noelle's shoulder. "Don't you be scaring her away."

Willis waved away Jake's concern. "No worries there, I hope." He looked to Noelle.

She smiled. "No, sir."

"Just call me Will," he said. "I hope to be able to welcome you to the family soon." He looked at the Christmas tree in the corner of the room. "If you don't find a Christmas star, I'll make sure you have one."

Tears stung Noelle's eyes. It felt so wonderful to be accepted by Jake's family. Alex's family had thought for a time that she was unworthy to become a Cabot.

Noelle spent the next day looking up job possibilities in the area. It tore at her heart to realize that going forward in a relationship with Jake would mean she'd have to leave her family and her patients at New Life behind.

While she was making notes about opportunities in the area, Jake called. "I've got to be away for a day or so. Business I have to take care of. I told Silas that you'd stop by. Okay?"

"Yes, I've already promised him that we'd spend time each day looking for our special star for the top of the Christmas tree."

"Thanks. I'll see you Christmas Eve. Remember, you're going to spend that evening and all the next day with my family."

"Yes. I'm already thinking of little gifts I can bring."

Noelle could hear the smile in his voice. "All we really need is you."

She clicked off the call and sat a moment letting a wave of happiness wash over her. She'd decided not to share her situation with her mother and father yet. And though she'd talked to her group of women at New Life, she hadn't mentioned it to them either. She told herself not to be superstitious, but she didn't want to say anything about her relationship with Jake until more time had passed.

Later that morning, she and Silas walked the beach. The wind off the water was cold and Silas was as ready as she when it was time to end their search. They'd decided they still had a little time to find what they were looking for.

Noelle opened one of her new cookbooks, searching for a dessert she could make for Christmas Eve. That, she decided, would be one of her gifts for the entire family. She just had to make sure it turned out right. She decided on an old-fashioned recipe called Snow Pudding. The jelled lemon, sugar and water mixture would be topped with a vanilla bean custard sauce. That's the part she was worried about. Cookbooks warned of overheating and "breaking" the sauce.

She was in the middle of making the sauce when her cell interrupted her. She stopped stirring the sauce and clicked on the call. At the sound of Jake's sexy hello, she grinned. She couldn't wait to see him again.

"Well, hello? How is your business trip going?"

"Very well. What are you doing?" he asked.

She shrieked, dropped the phone and went to the stove. The custard mixture was madly boiling. It looked awful. She pulled the pan off the stove and sighed at the thought of starting all over again.

"What's going on? Is everything all right?" asked Jake when she returned to the call.

"It will be. I'm cooking something, and it isn't going well."

"Need help?"

"No, thanks. I've got to do this on my own."

"I won't keep you. I just wanted to let you know I love you," said Jake.

"How sweet," she said, remembering how he'd told her that earlier. "I love you too. Can't wait to see you!"

"I should be there sometime tomorrow in the early afternoon. Save some time for me."

"That's an easy promise to make." She was still smiling when she clicked off the call. She gamely got more eggs out of the refrigerator.

CHAPTER TWENTY-ONE

The next morning Noelle awoke with a sense of expectation. Lemony sunshine shone through the window in her bedroom, beckoning to her. She put on her jogging clothes and headed out to the beach. Knowing she'd be seeing Jake later in the day made her feel wonderfully alive.

Jogging along the sand, she lifted her arms in the air, like she'd once done, feeling as if with a few extra flaps of her arms she could take flight. She hadn't mentioned to anyone that Christmas Day, was her birthday, and she wouldn't. She had enough to celebrate already.

As she ran, she studied the sand looking for the special item for the Christmas tree—something that would serve as a Christmas star in keeping with the theme of the tree. Will had assured her that he had something suitable if they didn't find what they wanted on the beach, so she decided not to worry about it. As long as Silas was satisfied, she would be too.

After returning to the house, she showered and dressed for her appointment at the day spa. In addition to getting her hair trimmed, she was going to enjoy a manicure and pedicure—a gift to herself.

Noelle left the cottage in a jovial mood. She already had books to give Silas for Christmas, and she was going to buy a bottle of champagne to accompany the dessert she was providing as her contribution to Christmas Eve dinner. The second batch of custard sauce had turned out fine. All she needed was a small crystal bowl to serve the sauce in and a gift for Jake.

At the day spa, Noelle reveled in being pampered. She'd been so busy with Silas and the Bellingham family that she hadn't bothered with her hair or her nails for a while.

When she explained why she was visiting the area, her hairdresser nodded. "It's good to make a clean break. I'm from Ohio originally, but I love living in Florida where I can get out on the beach with friends almost any day of the year."

"It's nice," agreed Noelle. She hadn't told her hairdresser everything, of course, but enough to value her encouragement. It had taken four amazing women to make Noelle move forward. Now it seemed so simple. And how valuable it was. When the time came to break the news of her relationship with Jake, they'd be among the first to know.

When she left the spa, Noelle all but danced into the mall to purchase the small serving bowl she'd seen earlier and to buy a gift for Jake. After much thought, she ended up buying him a pewter picture frame. It represented so many possibilities to her.

At the cottage, she wrapped her gifts and transferred the custard sauce into the newly washed crystal bowl. She decided to do some more investigation about the area online. At the sound of a knock at the door, she hurried to answer it.

She opened it and faced Jake. He was wearing a Christmas-red V-neck sweater and a smile that made her insides tingle.

"Welcome home!" she cried, throwing her arms around him.

His eyes glowed as he bent to kiss her. "Thought I'd never get here. Sometimes I hate flying. Want to walk along the beach with me while I stretch my legs?"

"Sure. Come in, and I'll get my jacket."

The sun that had awakened her that morning was still shining brightly as they walked along the beach. Sunlight tipped the edges of the waves rolling into shore making the scene sparkle like the crystal glass bowl she'd purchased as part of her surprise for his family.

"How was your trip?"

"That's what I want to talk to you about," said Jake. He grinned at her.

"All right," she said slowly. Jake was acting like a kid at Christmas.

Jake pulled her over to a spot away from the ocean, near an area of sea oats. He knelt in the sand and pulled a small, black-velvet box from his pants pocket.

"Noelle North, will you marry me? I don't want to wait any longer to make you a permanent part of my life. I can't imagine ever being without you. My son adores you, and I do too. In the short time I've known you, I realize what I've been missing all my life. You're everything I've ever wanted rolled up in the cutest, the bossiest, the most wonderful person I've ever met. I will be forever grateful if you say yes."

Surprise turned to tears of joy that rolled down her cheeks freely. She clasped his face in her hands and kissed him, her lips telling him her answer. When they parted, she said, "Yes, yes, and yes!"

He opened the box. A large, round diamond flanked by baguettes on either side winked up at her. The sun shone on it, sending light in all directions. Glancing at the streaks of refracted light, Noelle let out a gasp.

"Glad you like it," said Jake.

"No! Over there! Look! Our Christmas star!"

She raced over to the sea oats and from their growth pulled out the empty shell of a starfish. "This is what we've been waiting for! Silas will be thrilled!"

Jake laughed and held up the ring box. "What about this?"

She hurried to Jake's side and set down the starfish on the sand next to them. "I love it! I really do. And I promise to wear it always."

Jake slid the ring on her finger. "There. That's more like it."

Noelle smiled and held out her left hand, studying the ring that symbolized the life they would build together. "It's beautiful, Jake. I love it, but not as much as I love you." She clapped her hands together. "Oh my God! I have to call my parents."

"They already know," said Jake. "My business trip was to meet them and get their blessing. Your parents are great people who love you a lot, and they understand how anxious I am to make you mine." He gave her a sheepish look. "They put me through pretty much what my parents have done with you. I get it. Each of us has been hurt, and our families want to make sure we're going to be happy together. I guess I'd want to do the same thing for Silas."

"Can I just tell you that I think you're the best man I've ever met?"

"Your mother told me you were born on Christmas and you've always been her Christmas angel." He pulled her to him. "And now you're my Christmas angel. For now, and always."

He squeezed her tight. "I also went to see your friends at New Life. Aware that you'd be leaving them, I wanted to make sure they were all right with everything. They were thrilled their Plan A had worked out the way they wanted."

New tears threatened. "You did all that for me?"

His smile was tender as he reached for her. "I'd do anything for you."

Her heart filled and overflowed with love for him. She couldn't hold back her tears of joy.

"Are you all right," he asked, giving her a look of concern.

"I'm better than all right. With you, I'm the happiest woman in the world."

"Well, then, you'd better give me another kiss."

They were smiling as their lips touched.

At Althea's house, his parents were napping, giving Noelle and Jake privacy with Silas. When they showed Silas the starfish, he cried, "It's perfect!"

"And guess what, Silas," said Jake. "Look at Noelle's hand. We're engaged. She said yes. Noelle and I are going to be married, and she'll become your mother."

Silas threw his arms around Noelle's waist and hugged her hard. When he lifted his face, she saw tears in his eyes. "Now you can read my secret message to you." He turned to Jake. "Lift me up, Dad. I need to give it to her."

Jake held Silas in his arms and held him as high as he could.

Silas reached for the shell and took it in his hands. "Got it."

Jake lowered Silas to the ground and stood by while Silas handed Noelle her shell with his message attached.

"Here," said Silas. "It's from me."

With trembling fingers, Noelle began to unfold the note that had been attached to the shell.

"Hurry!" cried Silas, jumping up and down. "I want to tell you my secret!" He motioned for her to bend down.

Eyes sparkling with excitement, he whispered in her ear. "I love you."

Noelle hugged him and said, "I love you too, Silas. I always have."

She handed Jake the note. In bold letters, Silas had printed: "I love you, Noelle! Will you be my mom?"

Jake read the note and smiled at them, the rims of his eyes red from holding back tears. "I love the two of you more than you'll ever know."

"Are we a family now, Dad?"

He hugged Silas to him. "Yes, son, we are the happiest family I know."

"Now, Dad, put up the Christmas star. My wish came true."

Jake placed the starfish at the top of the tree and then stood back.

Smiling at her, Jake clasped Noelle's hand and put his arm around Silas's shoulder, and the three of them, bound together with the promise of their future, gazed up at their perfect Christmas star.

As a special Christmas gift to my readers, I'm including the recipe for Snow Pudding.

SNOW PUDDING

For the pudding:

2 envelopes plain gelatin

2/3 cup sugar

1/8 teaspoon salt

3 cups boiling water

¼ cup lemon juice

3 egg whites

¼ teaspoon cream of tartar

¼ cup sugar

1 tsp. grated lemon rind

Combine gelatin, sugar, salt in bowl, Add water and stir until ingredients are dissolved. Cool.

Add lemon juice and chill until syrupy (almost congealed).

Quickly beat egg whites and cream of tartar until soft peaks form. Add ¼ cup sugar slowly and beat until peaks are stiff.

Fold the stiff egg whites into the gelatin mixture and add lemon rind.

Fold carefully but completely so the effect makes the mixture look white like snow

Chill thoroughly until pudding is firm

Take the three leftover egg yolks and use them to make a custard sauce

CUSTARD SAUCE

For the sauce:

3 egg yolks

4 tablespoons sugar

Pinch of salt
1 cup of scalded milk
Flavoring to taste — usually vanilla, but can use any favorite liqueur or brandy

Heat water to a simmer in the lower part of a double boiler. Beat the egg yolks lightly and put them in the top section of the boiler with a pinch of salt and the sugar. Gradually add the scalded milk, stirring it in slowly with a wooden spoon. Cook and stir until the mixture begins to form a film or coating on the spoon. *Do not let the water boil.* As soon as the sauce coats the spoon slightly, take it from the hot water and pour into a cool bowl. *If this sauce is overheated or overcooked, it will curdle.*

Thank you for reading *A Christmas Star*. If you enjoyed this book, please help other readers discover it by leaving a review on Amazon, Goodreads, or your favorite site. It's such a nice thing to do.

Enjoy an excerpt from my book, *Going Home*– A Chandler Hill Book (Book 1 in the Chandler Hill Series, which will be out in early 2019.

CHAPTER ONE

In 1970, the only things Violet Hawkins wanted for her eighteenth birthday were to escape the Dayton, Ohio, foster-care system in which she'd been raised and to make her way to San Francisco. There, she hoped to enjoy a mellow lifestyle and find the love that had always been absent in her life.

Though she made it to San Francisco easily enough, she soon discovered she couldn't afford a clean, safe place in which to settle down. At first, it hadn't seemed to matter. Caught up in the excitement and freedom of living in a large city where free love and openness to so many things reigned, she almost forgot about eating and sleeping. One couch, one futon was as good as any other as long as grass or other drugs were available, and others didn't mind giving her a place to sleep. But after spending four months there, the dollars she'd carefully saved, which had seemed so many in Dayton, were nothing but a mere pittance in a city where decent living was too expensive for her. She took to wandering the streets with her backpack until she came upon a friendly group willing to give her a sleeping space inside or a bite to eat.

One June day, feeling discouraged, she'd just sunk down onto the steps outside a row house when a young man emerged.

He smiled down at her. "Tired?"

She was more than tired. She was exhausted and hungry. "Looking for work. I need to eat."

He gave her a long, steady, blue-eyed look. "What's your name?"

"Violet Hawkins. But call me Lettie."

His eyebrows shot up. "With all that red hair, no flowery name for you?"

She shook her head. She'd always hated both her hair and her name. The red in her hair was a faded color, almost pink, and the name Violet indicated a delicate flower. She'd never had the luxury of being the least bit frail.

He sat down beside her and studied her. "You don't look like the hippie type. What are you doing in a place like this?"

"On my eighteenth birthday, I left Dayton, Ohio, to come here. It sounded like a great plan—all this freedom."

"How long have you been here?"

"Four months. I thought it would be different. I don't know ... easier, maybe."

He got to his feet. "How about I fix you a sandwich, and then I'll tell you about a job, if you want it. It's at a vineyard in Oregon. I'm heading there later today."

Her glance slid over his well-built body, rugged facial features, and clean, shoulder-length, light-brown hair. He didn't fit into the usual crowd she'd been with, which made her cautious. "Who are you? And why would you do this for me?"

"Kenton Chandler." His lips curved into the same warm smile he'd given her earlier. "I'm heading to Oregon, and, frankly, I could use the company. Keeps me from falling asleep."

"Yeah? And what is this vineyard?"

He shrugged. "A couple of years ago, my dad bought a small inn with 75 acres of land in the Willamette Valley south of Portland. He's planted most of the land with grapes. He doesn't know that much about making wine and wants me to learn. That's why I'm in San Francisco. I've been working at a vineyard in Napa Valley just north of here, learning the ropes." He grinned. "Or maybe I should say, learning the vines."

"What kind of sandwich?" she asked, warming toward him and his wacky humor. Her stomach rumbled loud enough for them both to hear it.

"How does ham and Swiss sound?" he said, giving her a knowing look.

"Okay." Lettie didn't want him to think she couldn't manage on her own. That was dangerous. She'd learned it the hard way, fighting off a guy who thought he could have her just because he gave her a puff of weed. She'd been careful ever since to stay away from situations and guys like that.

"Well?" He waved her toward the door.

Lettie checked to see if others were within hearing range if she needed them. Plenty of people were hanging around nearby. Thinking it was safe, Lettie climbed the stairs behind Kenton. He didn't know about the knife tucked into one of the pockets of her jeans.

Inside, she found the same kind of contrast between this house and others she'd been in. It wasn't sparkling clean, but it was tidier than most.

He led her into the kitchen. "Sit down. It'll only take me a minute to make your sandwich." He handed her a glass of water. "Mustard? Mayo?"

"Both," she replied primly, sitting down at a small pine

table in the eating area of the room.

She sat quietly, becoming uncomfortable with the idea that he was waiting on her. She wasn't used to such a gesture. She was usually the one waiting on others both in her foster home and at the church where she'd spent hours each week attending services and events with her foster family. Thinking of them now, a shiver raced across her shoulders like a frightened centipede. It had been her experience that supposedly outstanding members of a church weren't always kind to those they'd taken into foster care primarily for the money.

"Ready!" said Kenton, jarring her out of thoughts of the past. He placed a plate with the sandwich in front of her and took a seat opposite her.

She lifted the sandwich to her face and inhaled the aroma of the ham. Keeping her eyes on Kenton, she bit into the bread, savoring the taste of fresh food.

He beamed at her with satisfaction when she quickly took another bite.

"Who lives here? Lettie asked.

"A friend of mine," said Kenton. His gaze remained on her. "You don't look eighteen."

She swallowed, and her breath puffed out with dismay. "But I am."

"And you're not into drugs and all the free-love stuff everyone talks about?"

Lettie shook her head. "Not really. I tried weed a couple of times, but it wasn't for me." Her strict upbringing had had a greater influence on her than she'd thought.

"Good. Like I said, if you want to ride to Oregon with me, there's a job waiting for you at the Chandler Hill Inn. We're looking for help. It would be a lot better than walking the streets of Haight-Ashbury. Safer too."

She narrowed her eyes at him. "And if I don't like it?"

He shrugged. "You can leave. One of the staff recently left for L.A. That's why my father called me to ask if I knew anyone who could come and work there. You're my only choice."

Lettie's heart pounded with hope. Acting as nonchalant as she could, she said, "Sounds like something I'd like to try."

The ride to Oregon was mostly quiet as an unexpected ease developed between them. Kenton answered any questions she had about him, the inn, and the way he thought about things. Lettie was surprised to learn he hadn't joined in a lot of the anti-war protests.

"My best friend died in 'Nam. He believed in serving our country. I want to honor him," he said to Lettie.

"A boy in my high school was drafted. His parents weren't happy about it."

"Well, if I'm drafted, I'm going," Kenton said. "I don't want to, but I will. I don't really have a choice."

As they talked, they agreed that John Wayne was great in the movie *True Grit*.

"And I love the Beatles," said Lettie.

"Yeah, me too. Too bad they just broke up."

"And what about the new group, The Jackson 5?" Lettie said.

"They're great. And I like Simon and Garfunkel and their music too."

At one point, Lettie turned to Kenton. "Sometimes you seem so serious, like an old man. How old are you, anyway?"

He gave her a sheepish look. "Twenty-two."

They shared a laugh, and in that moment, Lettie knew she'd found a person with whom she could be herself.

Lettie woke to someone shaking her shoulder. She stared into the blue-gray eyes of a stranger and stiffened.

"Lettie, we're here," said a male voice.

As she came fully awake, she realized Kenton was talking to her.

"Here at Chandler Hill?" she asked, rubbing the sleep from her eyes.

She looked out through the windshield of the Ford Pinto and gaped at the huge, white-clapboard house sitting on the top of a knoll like a queen overlooking her realm.

Lettie scrambled out of the car and stood gazing at the clean lines of the two-story building. Across the front, four windows offset by green shutters were lined up with identical windows below. Beneath a small, protective, curved roof, glass panels bracketed a wide front door, welcoming guests. To one side, a two-story wing had been added to the house.

Green, leafy bushes offset by an assortment of colorful flowers she didn't recognize softened the front of the building. As she walked closer, she realized between the main house and the addition a small, stone patio and private garden had been installed.

"Come on in," said Kenton. "There's a beautiful view from the back porch."

Feeling as if she were Alice in a different kind of Wonderland, Lettie entered the house. As she tiptoed behind Kenton, her gaze darted from the polished surfaces of furniture to gilt-edged mirrors to a massive floral bouquet sitting on a large dining-room table. It all seemed so grand.

Kenton led her to a wide porch lining the back of the house. Observing the rolling land before her and, in the distance, the hills crouching in deepening colors of green, Lettie's breath caught. The sun was rising, spreading a gold topping on the hills like icing on cake. She'd never seen anything so beautiful, so peaceful.

"Nice, huh?"

Lettie smiled and nodded.

At the sound of footsteps behind her, she whirled around.

A tall, gray-haired man with striking features similar to Kenton's said, "Welcome home, son."

They shook hands, and then the older gentleman turned to her. "And who is this?"

Shy, she stared at the man who seemed so familiar to her.

Kenton nudged Lettie.

Minding her manners, Lettie held out her hand as she'd been taught. "Lettie Hawkins. I've come for a job." A niggling feeling kept her eyes on him longer than necessary. When she could no longer stop herself, she blurted, "Aren't you Rex Chandler, the movie star?"

He smiled. "Yes, I am. But I've changed professions."

Lettie held back a chuckle of delight. A friend's mother had privately adored him.

"Why don't the two of you come into the kitchen," said Rex. "Mrs. Morley will want to talk to Lettie, and I need to talk to you, Kenton."

As Lettie followed the men into the kitchen, a woman hurried toward them, crying, "Kenton! Kenton! You're home at last!"

Laughing, Kenton allowed the woman to hug him. "You'd think I've been gone a year, Mrs. Morley."

"You almost were," she said, smiling and pinching his cheek. "And look at you! More handsome than ever."

Looking as if he couldn't wait for her to focus her attention elsewhere, Kenton said, "Mrs. Morley, I'd like you to meet Lettie Hawkins. She's here for a job."

Mrs. Morley's gaze settled on Lettie. "So, you like to work?"

"She likes to eat," said Kenton, bringing a smile to Mrs. Morley's full face.

"By the looks of it, Lettie, you could use more food," said Mrs. Morley. "Let's you and I talk about what kind of jobs you could do around here. I'm short-handed at the moment."

Kenton and Rex left the kitchen.

Mrs. Morley waved Lettie over to a desk in a small alcove in the kitchen. After lowering her considerable bulk into a chair, Mrs. Morley faced her. Her green eyes exuded kindness as she studied Lettie. Her gray-streaked brown hair was pulled back from her face and banded together in a ponytail, giving Lettie a good look at her pleasing features.

"Have a seat, dear."

Lettie sat in the chair indicated for her and clutched her hands. After seeing the small inn and the beautiful countryside, she desperately wanted the job.

"Where are you from, Lettie? And why in the world do you want to work here in the country? I'd think a pretty, young girl like you would want to be in a city having fun."

Lettie paused, unsure how to answer her. She'd thought she'd like living in the city, being free to do whatever she wanted. But after four months of doing just that, the excitement had worn off. She liked to know where she was going to sleep at night and when she'd next eat.

"Maybe I'm just a country girl at heart," she answered lamely. Her two best friends at home would scoff at her, but right now, that's how she felt.

"Well, that's what you'll be if you stay on. A lot of activity is taking place around here, what with people buying up turkey farms and the like, turning them into vineyards, but it *is* country. I hope it always will be." She leaned forward. "Know anything about cooking? Cleaning?"

"Yes," said Lettie. "I used to do both in my foster home. I

was the oldest of eight kids there."

"Eight? My land, that's a lot of kids to take in," said Mrs. Morley.

Lettie curled her lip. "It's a lot of money. That's why they did it."

"I see," said Mrs. Morley, studying her. "So how long have you been on your own?"

"Four months," said Lettie. "I was in San Francisco when I met Kenton."

"Such a good, young man. I've known him for a while now," Mrs. Morley said, sighing with affection. "You're lucky he found you. Why don't we start in housekeeping, see how it goes, and then maybe you can give me a hand in the kitchen."

"Okay," Lettie said, jumping to her feet. "Where should I put my things? I need to get them from the car."

Mrs. Morley gave her an approving look. "I like your eagerness. Let me show you to your room and then I'll give you a tour."

The north half of the front of the house consisted of a large, paneled dining room she'd seen earlier. The long mahogany table that sat in the middle of the room held seats for twelve. A summer flower arrangement consisted of pink roses and pink hydrangeas interspersed with white daisies and sat in a cut-glass vase in the middle of the table. Along one wall, above a service counter, an open cupboard made of dark wood stored coffee mugs, extra wine goblets, and water glasses. A coffee maker and a burner holding a pot of hot water sat on the marble counter. A bowl of sugar, a pitcher of cream, and a dish of lemon slices were displayed nearby. At the other end of the counter, a large plate of homemade, chocolate-chip cookies invited guests to take one.

"How many guests do you usually have?" Lettie asked.

"We have six guest rooms, so we have as many as twelve

people for the breakfast we serve. During the day, people come and go on their own, tasting wine at nearby vineyards or sightseeing. We offer a simple dinner to those not wishing to travel to restaurants at night." A look of pride crossed Mrs. Morley's face. "Sometimes my husband, Pat, grills out, or Rita Lopez cooks up Mexican food. Guests like these homestyle meals. In fact, we're becoming known for them."

Lettie's mouth watered. It all sounded so good.

Mrs. Morley led her to a sideboard, opened its drawers, and gave her a smile. "Let's see how well you polish silver."

Later, after being shown how, Lettie was working on the silverware when Kenton walked into the kitchen.

"Well? Are you going to stay?" he asked.

"Yes," Lettie said with determination. The whole time she'd been cleaning the silver she'd been able to gaze at the rolling hills outside. This, she'd decided, is where she wanted to be. It felt right.

About the Author

Judith Keim enjoyed her childhood and young-adult years in Elmira, New York, and now makes her home in Boise, Idaho, with her husband and their two dachshunds, Winston and Wally, and other members of her family.

While growing up, she was drawn to the idea of writing stories from a young age. Books were always present, being read, ready to go back to the library, or about to be discovered. All in her family shared information from the books in general conversation, giving them a wealth of knowledge and vivid imaginations.

A hybrid author who both has a publisher and self-publishes, Ms. Keim writes heart-warming novels about women who face unexpected challenges, meet them with strength, and find love and happiness along the way. Her best-selling books are based, in part, on many of the places she's lived or visited and on the interesting people she's met, creating believable characters and realistic settings her many loyal readers love. Ms. Keim loves to hear from her readers and appreciates their enthusiasm for her stories.

"I hope you've enjoyed this book. If you have, please help other readers discover it by leaving a review on Amazon, Goodreads, or the site of your choice. And please check out the Hartwell Women Series, the Fat Fridays Group, the Salty Key Inn Series and The Beach House Hotel Series. ALL THE BOOKS ARE NOW AVAILABLE IN AUDIO on Audible and iTunes! So fun to have these characters come alive!"

Ms. Keim can be reached at www.judithkeim.com And to like her author page on Facebook and keep up with the news, go to: https://www.facebook.com/pages/Judith-Keim/184013771644484?ref=aymt_homepage_panel.

To receive notices about new books, follow her on Book Bub - http://bit.ly/2pZBDXq

And here's a link to where you can sign up for her periodic newsletter!
http://eepurl.com/bZoICX

She is also on Twitter @judithkeim, LinkedIn and Goodreads. Come say hello!

Acknowledgements

Every book is a component of various exercises, different pieces of work, and a whole lot of cooperation between people to make it happen. The journey is challenging from the conception of an idea to the writing of it, the editing and proofing, the creation of a cover and the production of an audio book.

I'm so fortunate to have a supportive husband who has become an important part of the business both with the financials and as an editor, a content editor I love and totally trust, a book cover creator whose work I adore, and a wonderful narrator of my audio books who makes my characters come alive.

Thank you Peter, Lynn Mapp, Lou Harper, and Angela Dawe! I'm so grateful to each of you. Together, you are the perfect team!